Night Shift:
Book Three of The Gifted Series
By Ana Ban

Night Shift by Ana Ban

1.Romance 2.Fantasy 3.Paranormal

First Edition

Printed in the USA

ISBN 9781522007401

For Julio

THE ELEMENTAL FAMILY TREE

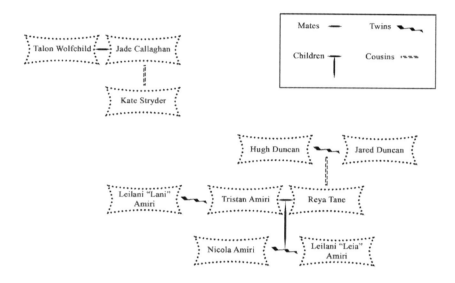

Talon Wolfchild — Jade Callaghan

Kate Stryder

Mates — Twins ▰

Children ┬ Cousins ▰▰▰

Hugh Duncan ▰ Jared Duncan

Leilani "Lani" Amiri ▰ Tristan Amiri — Reya Tane

Nicola Amiri ▰ Leilani "Leia" Amiri

Reese Valentine — Dominic Drake ▰ Emerson Drake

Juliet "Jinx" Desdemona ▰ Destiny "Desi" Desdemona

Jace Roake

Aden Collins

PREFACE

Life and death was only supposed to be something I wrote about. It wasn't right, experiencing it first-hand. And yet, there I was. Watching the man I loved, above all reason, bleeding to death on the floor. There was only one thing I could do.

Without thought, without reason, I crawled across the ground to his side. I was oblivious to the sharp rocks tearing into my flesh from the rough cement floor. My brain didn't comprehend the intense heat of the fire as it licked its way up the four walls of what had been my prison. I didn't notice my lungs constricting from the lack of oxygen in the smoke-filled room. Collapsing at his side, I tore open my own wrist and shoved the bleeding wound over his mouth.

It must work, I told myself. It *will* work.

CHAPTER 1

Nerves. They were almost tangible in the air as I examined myself in the mirror, putting on the final touches of the façade.

This wasn't the first time I'd played dress up and put on a good show, nor did I plan for it be the last. But for some reason, this time felt different. It felt like my life was about to change.

Shaking my head, I turned away from the mirror and found my shoes. It was the writer in me, it had to be. I wasn't normally this dramatic about things. Standing, I picked up my purse and headed out the door.

It was orientation day for Wilson's, and I had no idea what to expect. My nerves were still jumpy as I pulled into the lot and took in each sight, knowing I would record it all later. The sky above was a deep blue, a nice break from the week of rain we'd been having. There was still a chill to the air, something I was slowly becoming accustomed to in the Duluth spring. The parking lot was overflowing, being a favorite store among the locals.

I ran a hand along my shirt to smooth it, feeling the subtle lumps beneath it. It had taken me awhile to adjust to the extra weight, but, as all things I did, I knew it would be worth it.

With one last deep breath, I walked inside the store.

It was bright and clean, as all Wilson's were. That was partly the reason I chose this store- I knew that for the next 90 days, I could handle working here. The people, when I'd shopped in it before, were always friendly, the store always clean and I knew already that I would put my employee discount to good use.

Walking up to the service desk with my shoulders thrown back, I smiled at the young blonde behind the desk.

"Hi, I'm Reese Valentine. I'm here for orientation," I told her.

"Oh, great. Just follow this aisle down to the end of the registers, you'll see everyone else waiting there. Someone should be out soon and bring you back."

"Thanks!" I said brightly before heading down, wondering idly how many 'the rest' would be.

As promised, at the end of the aisle there were more- 15, after a quick head count, including me. Made sense, I figured, to hire quite a few at a time. We could all train together, make mistakes together and more than likely, they'd lose some before even the first week was up.

Most of the other recruits were men, as I expected. An overnight job of stocking didn't exactly shout feminine. There were two other females in the group, I was relieved to see, though I didn't mind working with men, either. I smiled at the girl next to me, who had short brown hair and pretty amber eyes.

"Hi, I'm Reese," I said.

"Becca," she replied shortly before turning to stare out the window.

Good start.

Another male joined our group, bringing the total to 16. I recognized him from the night I came in to do the interview. He was talkative that night, and I was happy to see he was hired too.

"Hey, Noah, right?" I asked.

"Yeah! What's your name again?" His smile was easy and reassuring after the cold reception Becca gave me, and it lit his azure eyes.

"Reese. You ready for this?"

"Oh, yeah, no problem."

A side door opened and a woman appeared, motioning us back. We followed dutifully through a large breakroom, complete with two fridges and a row of small appliances on a counter, and into another smaller room, set up with tables and a white board.

"Find your names," she instructed, "We're still waiting on a couple more, so it'll just be a few minutes."

I started down the second aisle and found my name in front of the third seat from the left. Noah sat in front of me, and good old Becca was on my right. The rest filed in, taking their seats, as we waited for it to begin.

The woman introduced herself as Abigail and told us to help ourselves to drinks and candy. I noted with amusement that there was a piece of chocolate attached to our binders already.

Half the people got up to grab sodas or water while I watched with interest. People watching had become one of the biggest aspects of my work, so I was pleased to see the odd assortment that was seated with me. Physically, no two looked the same. Personality wise, I'd have to wait and see.

Two more people walked in, but we still didn't begin. As I shuffled idly through the papers before me, *he* entered.

My heart literally skipped a full beat. As my mouth went dry, my eyes popped wide and stared as he neared my row, shuffled through to the front and leaned against the wall. When he passed by, the faintest whiff of his scent had my knees turning to liquid, and I was glad I was already seated. I realized I was staring but couldn't do anything to stop. His eyes took a slow perusal of the room without stopping on any one person.

My heart beat again, and I quickly looked into my lap where my fingers were tangled together and white knuckled. Making sure my mouth was closed, I snuck another look up under my lashes, maybe just to prove to myself that I could. His hair was dark, almost black, short and spiky, which accentuated the hard lines of his face. While most of the males in the room looked barely old enough to shave, he looked like a man. Tattoos flowed down his muscled arms from beneath a form fitting black shirt, and his jeans were faded and obviously well worn.

Looking down again, fiddling with the packets on the table, I tried to regain my breathing. No, I definitely had not imagined my first reaction. I was suddenly self-conscious, though he had not even spared me a glance. Ridiculous, I told myself. I'm here for a reason, and it is not to have my glands overreact.

Without conscious thought, I glanced up again. No, I didn't want to meet someone. But, damn, what was the harm in looking?

As if reading my thoughts, his head turned slowly and I was captured in his hard gaze. His eyes were a deep, glittering green, I realized erratically. While my eyes were locked on his, it felt as if everything else in the room dropped away. Noise vanished, colors dimmed and my breath stopped. Modern etiquette required that one of us look away, but I was helplessly locked in his depthless gaze. Chills ran down my arms and curdled in my stomach, making the butterflies I'd been feeling all day seem tame.

Just as slowly, he turned his head back to the front without so much as a change of expression. My eyes shot immediately down again, embarrassment firing into my cheeks. I blew out a breath, not sure if it was in relief or frustration.

Thankfully, Abigail began talking and I was under a short reprieve. After a brief introductory speech, she introduced *him*.

4

"With us today is Dominic Drake, he's one of your overnight managers," Abigail said, gesturing towards the man in the corner. He turned his gaze out over the small crowd, nodded once in acknowledgement, and faced back to Abigail.

Though my heart continued to beat erratically, I used all my will power to pay attention to what the woman was saying, the material on the table, and the few short videos we were made to suffer through.

At the end of orientation was the big tour of the store. As a group, we walked through the main part of the building, which was still relatively busy for as late as it had gotten. Abigail pointed out each section, but I was barely listening. *He* was walking in front of me, oblivious to my existence. I couldn't help but watch the way his snug jeans hung from his hips, and the way his tight shirt stretched across the muscles of his back. Tattoos peeked out from beneath the sleeves, and I tried, however conspicuously, to figure out what designs he'd had emblazoned on his person.

There were several symbols I didn't recognize; at first glance, I took them to be Chinese Kanji, but they weren't as detailed. Japanese, perhaps? The little I knew of that language didn't seem quite right, either.

I was staring so hard at the elegant swirls that, when he stopped suddenly, I plowed directly into his back.

Mortified, I stumbled back, a hand covering my mouth. Wide eyes met his incredulous ones. Before I could speak, to apologize or attempt to explain, Abigail glanced over at us.

"Everything okay over there?"

Dominic's dark gaze bore into mine, and I felt trapped under his glare. A willing prisoner, feasibly, but a prisoner just the same. When she spoke, however, he abruptly looked away. "Fine."

5

Swallowing once, my eyes shot to the floor once they were released. Fire burned in my cheeks for the second time today. As the group began to walk again, I surreptitiously found my way to the back, keeping a good distance between myself and the person in front of me.

We toured the back room, during which I managed to studiously avoid any more encounters with *him*. No matter how much I wanted otherwise.

I went home, knowing my first day had been something of a failure. Besides my botched attempt at talking to Becca and my brief interaction with Noah, I was silent and hardly even observant. *He* threw me off. I knew it was true, but it didn't make me feel any better. I was unprepared for the attack on my system. Well, next time I would be ready, I promised myself that.

It was late evening when I arrived home and fixed dinner, prepared to stay up for the night. The next night would be my first as an overnighter, and I wanted to get into the routine while I could. I didn't sleep much as it was, so I was hoping the schedule would be easy for me to fall into.

After a quick pasta meal, I sat down ready to begin writing. I wasn't nearly as excited as normal at the idea of a fresh page, and found my thoughts drifting way too often towards *him*. It was a look, *one* look, I admonished myself. Okay, two looks. And a brief contact with hard muscle that left me breathless. I desperately needed to let it go and concentrate.

I began writing and an hour later began to read through the first draft. This book was going on a little bit different genre than my previous works. I chose a night job because I was delving into something I'd always been interested in but too chicken to write about- vampires. The main character, Sydney, had been on her own since she was 18, traveling the world and losing all contact with family. After getting into some trouble in

6

Europe, she comes home to stay with the one family member who will still talk to her, her sister. She told everyone she was helping her sister out, babysitting her niece and nephew while her sister worked, but the truth was, she was running away from the trouble she'd gotten into. To keep her head down, she takes a job on the night shift.

Low and behold, she meets a man who can only come out at night.

I like to experience the things I write about. Fortunately, I have no ties in any one place, so if I wanted to write about a waitress living in the Greek Isles, I could take off and live it. Or, in this case, moving to the chilly town of Duluth to work overnight and write about vampires. Each book I wrote, minus the romance I inevitably put in, was like my own personal journal. I'd decided to wear a bodysuit for extra weight, curious how it would change people's interaction with me, if at all. Changing my hair color was easy- though, for this one, I left it my natural mousy brown. Same with eyes, though I again left them the same, which were the color of milk chocolate.

I sat back, reading the section of Sydney's first meeting with her mystery man. With a small frown, I realized I'd described *him*. Not exactly what I'd wanted for Sydney, but there it was. Shrugging, I continued on, knowing no one knew me better than my subconscious. And when I got into my writing zone, my subconscious tended to take over.

During the next day, I managed to catch a few hours of sleep before obsessing over what to wear to my first night of work. I dressed in the customary blue, though we were allowed at night to wear any type of bottoms instead of the black pants the day crew had to. Carefully I put on the padded suit, a blue shirt that tied in the back and flared out from the waist down, and a pair of jeans.

Deciding Sydney was a subtle kind of beauty, I put on just the minimal of makeup and left my hair to hang straight and long. Satisfied, I threw on a jacket, picked up my bag and headed out.

The small house I'd rented for the duration was tidy, with a well-kept lawn in front and a wooded area in back. It made me smile as I walked out and studied the night sky, filled with stars and a half moon. I'd spent most of my time on the coasts, and the change coming into central US was surprising. Not just the scenery, though it was wildly different than the deserts or ocean towns I'd always found so appealing, but the people themselves.

In the two weeks since I'd rented the house and interviewed for my newest job, I managed to spend plenty of time getting to know the city itself. Most people I spoke to grew up in or around Duluth, with a couple being as far away as Minneapolis. Perhaps because of that, I found that a lot of those people had a very small view of the world. I considered myself lucky that I'd been able to experience so many things in my life, but hanging out here made me additionally grateful that was true.

Food, for instance. The only Italian food was at the Olive Garden, which also doubled as the only fine dining restaurant in the area. Then there was sushi. After living in San Francisco about a year back, I had become a big fan of sushi. Driving around town here, I spotted only one sushi place.

It was attached to the back of a gas station.

Minneapolis was only a couple hours away, I had to remind myself more than once. There was bound to be a better selection there, if the need became too great.

I imagined Sydney would be feeling the same frustration, after living abroad. Perhaps even more so, because she grew up here and left. Coming back to this would be difficult.

At least for me, the novelty of living in a smaller town should keep me from going crazy too soon.

I held on to that thought as I approached the side door at Wilson's and rang the bell. It was after hours now, so I had to enter through the 'employee's only' door. After being buzzed in, I was greeted by who I assumed to be another night manager.

"Good morning," he smiled pleasantly. I smiled back at the joke.

"Hi. I'm Reese."

"Jacob. Nice to meet you," he said before turning to the woman leaning against the counter next to him. "This is Sandra, we're both managers. JR is going to show you what to do," he assured me, motioning towards a young guy across the room.

After nodding hello to Sandra, I walked over to join the group surrounding JR. He went through how to use the lockers, how to punch in and what we would be doing that day. If my eyes shot to the door every time I heard it buzz, I told myself I was only curious about who was coming in. I wasn't looking for *him*. Anyway, as a manager, he would be here by now.

My group of trainees consisted of three guys and me. We followed JR to the floor, where he showed us how to read the information on the boxes of freight that were coming in. After a couple of minutes, he set us loose to try it on our own.

We started in the section of dry food. When pallets of boxes were dropped off, we picked up the boxes and put them in the aisles. After that, we opened the boxes and stocked the shelves. While it was definitely a physical job, the mental capacity of the workers obviously didn't need to be too high.

We worked mostly in silence. There wasn't even music playing overhead, and for some odd reason I had a cartoon theme song stuck in my head. By the time our first break was called, I thought I was going to go insane.

Noah was working a few aisles down from me, so we walked together to the breakroom. He was the friendliest person I'd met so far. It made me wonder if this was typical for Duluth, or if a certain personality chooses to work overnight.

Noah was chattering on about unimportant things while we made our way to the breakroom. I did my best to respond correctly with a smile or laugh, sometimes even a comment, but he didn't seem to need much encouragement.

As we followed the rest of the group towards the double doors, I noticed most of the regular employees had wires sticking out of their ears, tucked into their shirts.

"Are we allowed to listen to music?" I asked Noah hopefully.

"I think so," he said. "I've seen a lot of people with headphones."

"Would have been nice for them to tell us that before we started," I grumbled.

"Yeah, right?" Noah agreed.

As we entered the breakroom, I realized I was still searching for *him*. It was a pretty good chance that he was working and I just hadn't seen him. After all, the store was very large and I'd been in one small section of it since I'd arrived. But once I realized I was searching every face for his, I forced myself to stop.

"So, do you go to college here?" Noah was asking me.

"No, I'm staying with my sister. I babysit my niece and nephew during the day. Are you in college?" The story came out smooth.

"Yeah. One more year to go."

"Congrats," I told him. We reached the lockers and I unlocked mine to get change for the soda machine. When I turned to go into the breakroom, a solid mass was blocking my way.

The smell registered first, and my eyes slowly lifted to look into those blazing green ones that had taken over my thoughts for the last 24 hours.

"Um. Hi," I managed, feeling like an idiot.

"Hi." His voice was deep and rough and set the butterflies winging.

We were mere inches apart, a fact which every part of my body was aware of. His eyes never left mine.

"Excuse me," he finally said, and lifted one brow mockingly.

"Oh. Oh!" I repeated, realizing he was trying to get to the desk behind me. "Sorry," I mumbled, and scooted around him and into the breakroom.

Stupid, stupid, stupid, I repeated over and over in my head. I stood in front of the soda machine, regulating my breathing and attempting to focus. As quickly as was possible, I shoved the change in and got a water back. I chose a chair across from a guy using the 15 minutes to sleep and tried to disappear.

I saw him enter from my peripheral and sit at a table two down from me. Noah was at another table laughing with a group from our orientation. Normally this would be my time to observe and gauge; as it was, I stared at my water bottle and focused on getting under control.

My stomach was still jumping when they called our nightly meeting directly after break. I half listened to the numbers the three managers rattled off and only snapped out of it when I heard that raspy voice again.

"We have some new recruits tonight. Why don't you all introduce yourselves."

My head shot up as he gestured towards a guy in front.

"I'm Will, born and raised in Duluth."

As I realized all the new members were introducing themselves, his eyes met mine and I felt my heart beat unsteadily again. Just like the first time, our gaze held for more than was considered polite. I heard some snickering and managed to focus on what was being said.

"It's your turn, Reese," Jacob was saying, obviously not for the first time. My eyes switched from Dominic to Jacob and I felt color rising in my cheeks.

"I'm Reese," I managed quietly.

He quirked a smile. "Where you from, Reese?"

My mind blanked. Where was I from. Where was I from?

"Uh... San Francisco, most recently."

That wasn't my back story. Oh, crap, I realized too late, when I interviewed my last job was written down as being in Tampa. What was I thinking?

12

But it didn't seem to faze Jacob. He moved on to the next person, having them introduce themselves. I stared down at the bottle of water again, fiddling with the label until, finally, they released us.

I shot out of the room, not bothering to stop at the locker to put away the water and not waiting for Noah either. When I reached the aisle I was working, I put my head down and immediately began tearing open boxes. It was humiliating to be so flustered, especially when all the man did was look at me.

Dominic. He was now the bane of my existence.

CHAPTER 2

The next two hours of my shift I spent working diligently and memorizing the process. Mostly we were left to our own devices, only being shown something briefly before being sent off to work. That was fine by me, for obviously I wasn't ready for interaction. Noah talked to me every now and again, but otherwise the night was spent in silence.

Lunch time, which was odd to think of 3:00 in the morning as lunchtime, was taken as a group like all breaks would be. Since the store was closed, we were locked in at night, and taking breaks together made it easier to keep track of everyone.

I sat at the same table, with the same tired companion, and munched on a protein bar. This time, though, I was determined to get some work done. Instead of torturing myself by looking Dominic's way, I scanned the other half of the room. What I saw turned my stomach.

Bags of chips, two-liter sodas and other assortments of junk food seemed to be the norm. A lunch of that caliber was bad enough in the daytime; at 3:00 AM, it seemed unusually awful.

There were a few people heating up remnants of a past dinner, or those lovely microwaveable trays that looked like mush and tasted like cardboard. The smells emanating from the direction of the microwaves was nauseating. I set down the bar I was eating and concentrated instead on not being sick. It was crowded in the room, as it had been during the first break, but adding on the noise and smells made my head spin.

Hugging both arms to my stomach, I took a few deep breaths. It only made the spinning worse. I had to get out, was all I could think. I needed to breathe.

Lunging out of the chair, I shot out of the breakroom door and moved quickly down the hallway. I burst out into the main check lanes and made a beeline for the bathroom. Once inside, I braced myself with both hands on the sink and took deep breaths. Once that was under control, I ran a paper towel under cold water and wiped it across my face and neck, trying to cool off. When I studied my reflection, I saw circles under my eyes and the stringy mess my hair had become.

Shaking my head, I grabbed a hair tie out of my pocket and did some fast work to fix that mess. The eyes would have to do, since I didn't have any makeup on me, but I pinched my cheeks to add some color. Satisfied, I headed slowly back for the breakroom.

It wasn't often I got claustrophobic. Actually, if I was being honest, it wasn't often I put myself in a situation that would cause me to be claustrophobic. It had been so long since I'd been in a large group, I had almost forgotten it was a trigger. It was odd, and a weakness, but one I had to deal with. Small spaces didn't really bother me so much, per se, but feeling closed in did. Perhaps that was why I preferred the desert, or the ocean. So much space was to be had in either place. For a very short stint I'd spent time in Portland, and I found that it was difficult for me there, even outside. The trees were so huge and when I looked to the horizon, I couldn't see it. All I saw were trees.

I was beginning to have serious doubts about my choice of profession for the next three months. If it was this bad my first night, would it get any better? The people were unfriendly, the breakroom made me sick and *him*...

I didn't know what to do about Dominic.

My face lifted towards the breakroom, and I stopped dead in my tracks. Speaking of the devil, there he stood, a dark figure in the doorway. He was staring at me, unmoving and silent. With a gulp, I reached out with one hand and gripped the railing beside me.

16

He turned, and I was released from the odd effect he had on me. Shaking my head to clear it, I moved on.

Next to me I heard chatter and it took me a moment to realize it was Spanish, not English. I understood it just fine- languages came easily to me, and I was fluent in both Spanish and French- it just surprised me to hear it in this area. Duluth wasn't exactly a cultural hub.

I glanced over and smiled at the cleaning crew, made up of three men and one woman, all looking from Hispanic descent.

"You okay?" One of the men asked in halting English.

"*Too many white people. Made me sick to my stomach*," I responded in Spanish with a grin, putting my hand over my stomach and making a face. All four of them burst out in laughter.

"*Any time you need to get away from them, come sit with us*," the same man told me.

"*I just might. Have a good night*," I winked and walked back the rest of the way.

Well, it seemed that there were at least a few normal people here.

After lunch, we went back to the same work. My feet began to hurt, and I realized I probably wasn't wearing the proper shoes. I remembered hearing somewhere that boots were better for working on concrete floors than tennis shoes were. I'd worn no-slip soles, thinking that best, but in the future, I was definitely going for comfort.

With just an hour remaining of the shift, I suddenly felt the hair on my arms raise and my heart beat just a little bit quicker. Before looking up, I knew who the shadow belonged to that was overtaking my aisle.

"Hello, Reese," he said in that deep voice that sent butterflies tumbling in my stomach.

"Hello. Dominic, isn't it?" I thought I managed to sound rather blasé.

"That's right," he quirked his mouth in what could be counted as a smile. "Enjoying your night so far?"

"Such a blast," I told him, straight faced. "I really feel challenged and intellectually stimulated."

The smile was full on this time, if only for a moment. I was amusing him.

"Are you feeling all right? I saw you run off to the restroom during lunch."

His concern had me stuttering. "Er… yeah, I'm fine. Just not used to staying up all night, and the smells in the breakroom made me a little queasy. No biggie," I finished lamely.

He studied me with those deep emerald eyes as if judging my soul. In an abrupt change of topic, he asked, "What'd you do before? You said you were from San Francisco?"

I shrugged. Damn. I had to do some back tracking to fix my blunder. "One in a long list of cities. I actually lived in Tampa before here, but it was so short a time I sometimes forget."

There, that should help smooth things over.

"Why do you move so much?" He asked, his eyes staring hard into mine. It took me a second to swallow.

"I… like adventure."

"Do you now," he said so lowly, I couldn't be sure if it was actually to me.

18

We stood awkwardly for a minute before he took a step away. "If you have any questions, feel free to come to Jacob or myself."

I nodded, watching him leave. And went back to stocking pet food.

When I got home that morning, my feet hurt so bad I was nearly limping inside. It was a cool morning, though the sun shone brightly. Sticky with sweat, I immediately stripped down, taking care with the bodysuit, and stepped into a hot shower. Letting the grime of the night slough off, I stayed in the shower longer than the hot water lasted, letting the heat work on the soreness of my muscles. If it weren't for my aching feet and severely lacking water heater, I would have stayed in there all day.

Luckily, the bodysuit was machine washable, so I started a load after wrapping myself in a fluffy robe. After that, I set to work filling a bucket with soapy water, after boiling some since I'd run out of hot water, and a special relaxing mixture that was supposed to draw out toxins from the skin. Setting it below my computer desk, I sank into the chair with a bowl of cereal in my lap. It wasn't what I wanted to eat, but it was the simplest.

Sinking my feet into the hot water, I relaxed into the seat with a sigh. Shoe shopping was definitely on my agenda today, if I could wake up in time. I looked longingly towards the bedroom, with the soft comforter and blackout curtains, but forced myself to focus. I wanted to write my impressions from my first night before I gave in to my exhaustion, before I lost them.

As I began writing, I found my mind drifting much more often than normal. Dominic's eyes were the star of my daydreams. They were so intense, every time he locked his gaze with mine I felt as if I were sinking and floating simultaneously. Like he had his own gravity, and I was being sucked into it, yet there was a forcefield holding me back.

What is this, Star Wars? I asked myself sardonically.

Shaking my head in an attempt to dislodge the distracting thoughts, I set to work again, giving up 20 minutes later when my brain decided to dissect every action Dominic had made during the night. Every smirk, each lingering look. Words left unsaid.

Pulling my feet out of the cooled bucket, water slopping over the edge, I wiped them off quickly with a towel before sending the remains down the drain. I was being ridiculous. I was nothing to this man, and I needed to shut it down before I lost all focus. Shoving an oversized shirt over my head, I crawled into bed and went to sleep.

Unfortunately, my subconscious now had control, and just as when I was awake, my mind couldn't stay away from thoughts of *him*.

It was dark in the forest, lit only by the full moon. As I wandered down the path, I realized immediately that it was familiar. I was in my back yard.

While I wandered, I began to smell each distinct scent, began to see individual colors that had not been visible before. I could sense more than see the smaller animals skittering away as I veered into their path.

I felt no sense of urgency as I meandered through the trees, enjoying the beauty of nature. Pausing, I placed a hand briefly on a fallen tree, a sense of loss overwhelming me.

Just then, I realized I wasn't alone. Turning slowly, a hand still against the rough bark, I came eye to eye with Dominic.

"What are you doing here?" I asked, my voice as soft as the breeze.

"I'm here for you," he answered me, his voice seeping through my skin.

His tattoos moved then, hypnotic in their dance. My eyes riveted to them, I felt myself swaying in time to their beat. The ground felt as if it had fallen away, but I didn't mind. I was floating.

When I blinked, the spell was broken, and Donovan was gone. In his place stood a majestic gray wolf.

Waking in the early evening, I cleared my mind of the haziness of dreams. Instead of feeling groggy, as I expected after sleeping in the day, I felt unusually awake and optimistic. After getting dressed and wolfing down breakfast, I headed to the mall.

My first stop was a small shoe store, which displayed boots of all varieties. It looked promising, and as soon as I stepped inside, I had two salesmen at my beck and call.

After explaining my dilemma, within a few minutes I had piles of boxes along either side of the chair they'd had me sit in. One even tied my shoes for me, which felt both ridulous and luxurious.

"These have the tennis shoe style, but a hiking boot bottom," one was explaining to me. "Boots are great, until you need to squat down. These would give you more freedom of movement, without losing the sole that you need."

Taking a lap around the store, I smiled at my helpers. "Sold."

On my way out of the store, I strolled down, taking a look around at what else the mall had to offer. There was a chocolate shop that smelled divine, but I kept walking.   When I reached a children's store, an idea struck.

Part of my story was that I was watching kids in the daytime, kids that would still need car seats.   Inspired, I headed into the store and purchased two of the cheapest models I could find.   Once I was done, I could always donate them to a good cause.

Satisfied with my purchases, I made my way to the parking lot.   It was almost time for work.

CHAPTER 3

New shoes on my feet, I walked confidently into Wilson's a few minutes before I needed to clock in. New shoes, new attitude. I wouldn't let some insanely sexy man distract me from my true purpose any longer.

Though we were still loosely being trained, I hadn't forgotten anything from the night before, and JR left us to our own devices. While I tore into a box full of chips- my new favorite aisle, since the boxes were so light- Jacob found me.

"Would you mind heading to softlines? We had a call-in, they could use an extra hand."

"Softlines?" I asked dumbly, sure that term had been used during orientation but unable to recall what it meant.

"Uh, clothes. Just walk down the middle here, you won't miss them."

Abandoning my aisle, I followed his directions, through home goods, and immediately understood what he meant when I hit the carpeted area that signaled I'd arrived at the clothing section.

At least 40 carts were lined up along either side of the main aisle, and one girl was throwing plastic covered fabric into random carts quicker than the men throwing fish in the market in Seattle. She had strawberry blonde hair and a deadly focused stare, and I hated to interrupt her rhythm.

"Excuse me," I called out. She didn't stop, just grunted in response. "I'm here to help."

She paused for only a moment, long enough to give me a once over.

"Great," she beckoned me over, and I walked to her side. With a finger, she pointed to each cart in succession.

23

"Tops, plus size tops, pants, shorts, bras, underwear, fancy pants, socks..."

"Fancy pants?" I asked, raising a brow.

In response, she walked to the cart and held up a scrap of lace. "Fancy underwear. They have their own bins."

"People wear those?"

"Apparently, not everyone has as glamorous a job as we do."

I liked her already. "I'm Reese," I told her.

"Jordan," she answered. "You started yesterday?"

"Yup," I responded. "How long have you worked here?"

"Three fun-filled years," she smirked. "Longer than I ever thought I would."

Jordan continued listing off what each cart held, then went back to tossing. While she did that, I grabbed one of the carts that had gotten full, replacing it with an empty one, and began ripping off the plastic and refolding the clothing inside. Since I wouldn't be much help sorting, and by the way Jordan worked it was a better chance I'd just be in her way, I did what I could to help the process.

The night moved much quicker doing this than lugging heavy boxes, and I found myself hoping to be permanently placed in this section. Jordan was fun to work with, constantly making little asides that had me giggling on more than one occasion.

After the truck was done being offloaded, a third person joined us. The bleach blonde woman, who looked a few years older than myself, was named Anita. I remembered her from the breakroom the night before, but hadn't actually spoken to her.

She was quieter than Jordan, with the sleepy countenance expected of an overnight worker. When I asked Anita how long she'd done this job, she told me she'd been at it for five years, which made me cringe. That seemed like a long time to do a job that was so obviously making her miserable.

I found myself more drawn to Jordan, who, while having worked here a substantial amount of time, hadn't succumbed to the drama and negativity I'd gotten a glimpse of yesterday, and which Anita seemed to be the living embodiment of. Jordan still had a sarcastically positive outlook, and I could tell she was also perfectly happy being left alone. If I weren't in a lie about most aspects of my life, we could become great friends.

Just before our first break time, while Jordan was showing me how to properly fold jeans, the hair suddenly raised along my neck and arms. Stiffening, I set the jeans carefully in their slot before turning.

"Ladies," Dominic greeted. "How is everything over here?"

"Great," Jordan answered for us. "She's a quick learner."

"Clothes are certainly preferable to pet food," I added.

The corner of his mouth tipped up. I took that to mean I was amusing him again.

"Good to know," he remarked before wandering off.

As soon as he was out of earshot, I blew out a breath. It didn't go unnoticed.

"What is it?"

Putting my focus on my task, I told her, "Nothing. It's just... he's a little intimidating."

"And hot," Anita popped up next to us. "But stay away."

25

Surprise flitted across my face as I looked at her. "Why?" I didn't think Anita had any claim on him, she'd been talking about her boyfriend all night. Not that it mattered if she did; I didn't have any claim on him either.

"He's trouble," Anita responded, as if it was obvious.

"I don't think any of those rumors are true," Jordan rolled her eyes.

"What rumors?" I couldn't help the curiosity in my voice, and hoped it didn't give me away.

Both girls looked at me knowingly, and I realized I had to be more careful.

"He's a total player," Anita stage whispered. "Kris told me."

"I trust Kris as far as I can throw her," Jordan tossed back. "The truth is probably that he turned her down, and she's spreading rumors to get back at him."

"That could be true," Anita agreed. "Most of the girls here have tried."

"Tried what?" I piped in.

"To hit that," Anita stated as if it should be obvious. "Working overnights doesn't exactly open up our social calendars," she continued. "So, when there's eye candy, there's normally a line."

I pondered the information while we walked towards the breakroom. Jordan plopped down in front of a table by the cash registers, not in the breakroom. Pausing, letting Anita walk by, I approached her slowly.

"Are we allowed to sit out here?" I asked her.

"Not really," she shrugged. "But, since it's just me, I've never been told not to."

Hesitating just a moment longer, I asked, "Would you mind if I sat with you?"

She shrugged again. "It's a free country."

"I'm just going to grab a water," I told her, though I didn't think she cared.

Rushing inside towards the vending machine, I stuck in my dollar, selected the water and headed back out before the smells assaulted me. Though Jordan didn't know it, she was now my safe haven.

Slipping thankfully into the chair across from her, I realized she had a book in front of her and was snacking on pistachios. Not wanting to disrupt her, I pulled out my phone, grateful for the invention of e-readers. I'd even brought headphones tonight, with my phone loaded up with music and audiobooks, though with Jordan's company, I hadn't needed either.

"What are you reading?" She asked suddenly.

"A sci-fi series," I told her the series name. It was my favorite fiction genre, and this particular series was one I'd read more than once.

"I've read a couple of those," she wrinkled her nose. "It got a little creepy about the fourth book in."

"It does," I agreed laughingly. Leaning closer, I told her, "I heard the author was off his meds when he wrote that one." She laughed too, and I leaned back. "But, if you can get through that, the seventh book in the series was by far the best."

Pondering that, she put a finger to her lips. "Maybe I'll give it another try, just skip the one I didn't like."

"Totally worth it," I agreed.

We lapsed back into easy silence, and I became doubly grateful to Jacob for sending me to softlines.

After 15 minutes, Jordan and I walked inside to listen in on the nightly meeting. The only managers tonight were Jacob and Dominic, and I found myself watching Dominic from my spot against the side of the wall. His eyes roamed over the crowd, never settling for more than a moment. When they brushed across me, I felt a tingle down to my toes. Did I imagine the longer pause as his eyes met mine? Before I could decide, they were on the move again.

I let out a little sigh, forgetting Jordan beside me. She nudged me, giving me a small smile when I glanced at her. Across the room, at a table with her boyfriend, Anita sat, not paying any attention as Jacob talked. Doing a quick scan of the rest of the faces, I listed off the names I knew in my head.

Noah wasn't around tonight, and only about half of the people I'd trained with last night were here. Since I had the next three nights off, I was guessing the managers wanted us trained, but also didn't necessarily need all of us working yet. It was still early for their busy season- JR had explained to us that as soon as summer hit, the work load would double.

After we were dismissed, I brought my water with me to the floor. I'd noticed both Jordan and Anita had water bottles with them at all times, and it seemed easier to keep track of in the clothing department than in the frenzied food area.

Free of the breakroom once again, I walked with Jordan back to the clothing section.

"He was staring at you, you know," Jordan commented.

Glancing sharply at her, I asked, "What do you mean?"

"Dominic, right when we walked into the meeting. I've never seen him take an interest like that before."

"I wouldn't necessarily call that 'taking an interest,' maybe I just had food in my teeth or something," I attempted to discourage any thoughts in that direction.

Jordan gave me a sideways look. "You didn't eat anything during break."

My mouth popped open to answer, but Anita managed to catch up with us, bubbling over with gossip once again. Jordan and I stopped talking, and her sudden silence strengthened my earlier thought that we could be good friends.

Anita started in on two of our coworkers who had gotten into a screaming match over in the towel aisle. Not recognizing their names, I zoned out until a tantalizing morsel snapped me back.

"...Dominic's apparently hand picking a team to work only in the fresh food," Anita rose a brow at us. "I guess they've had a lot of complaints from the day team about things not being rotated properly, so the bosses decided to train a specific team instead of just throwing anyone over there."

"That makes sense," I piped in. Realizing the two girls just stared at me, I wondered where my misstep was. "I've worked in food before," I allowed one shoulder to raise and drop, shrugging off my comment. "There's a lot to it, avoiding cross contamination, proper temperatures, amount of time things can be out of the coolers, that sort of thing."

"Sounds horrible," Anita commented.

"I don't know, it might be a nice change of pace," Jordan argued lightly. "Not that I would want to do that *every* night."

"I like it here," I was quick to add. "Think they'll let me work with you guys all the time?"

"Probably not," Jordan frowned. "The ladies over here are a bit territorial."

"Kind of sexist, having only women working in clothing," I tried to lighten the mood.

"Don't tell them," Jordan stage-whispered. "Can you imagine some of these guys having to put away the fancy pants?"

We all three shuddered, before Anita walked back to where she had been working before break.

Jordan and I worked silently after that, and I slipped in one earbud to listen to a book on tape. The Count of Monte Cristo was loaded up, and I easily got lost in the story. Even though I had one ear open, my only warning were the little raised hairs on the back of my neck, and I still managed to jump as the voice intruded.

"Good book?" Dominic's voice was amused.

I glared at him, yanking the earbud out. "How did you know I was listening to a book?"

"I could hear it," he motioned towards the hanging bud, then quickly changed the topic. I hadn't thought it was that loud. "How are things going over here?"

"Fine, good," I answered, struggling for a response. "We, uh, we have 12 carts left to put away."

Jordan appeared from the side, rescuing me. "We should be done by 5:00," she told him helpfully. "Anita and I can backstock."

Not sure what that meant, I glanced back to Dominic as he spoke. "Great, I could use some help. Reese, why don't you come find me when you're wrapped up here?"

"Where will you be?" I asked.

"The coolers. Jordan can show you."

"That's great!" Jordan piped in. "Reese has experience in fresh food."

Floundering, I looked between the two.

"I'll keep that in mind," Dominic's voice had dropped, his eyes focused solely on me.

My mouth went dry.

"I'll see you at 5:00," he murmured before walking away.

Jordan grinned at me once he was out of earshot. "You're welcome."

CHAPTER 4

Lunch was a relaxing half hour, munching on my salad and losing myself in the same book from my first break, while Jordan half read and half napped across from me. The cleaning crew, who I'd met briefly the night before, also lounged at the tables near us.

I'd greeted them when I first sat down, and asked each of their names. Pedro, Enrique and Juan were the men, while Rosalita, Rosa for short, was the woman. After introducing myself, I slid into my seat and let out a breath.

Whether it was the new shoes, or the slight extra padding the carpet afforded, my feet were nowhere near as sore as the night before, though the relief when I sat down was still palpable. For a few minutes, I extended them out, stretching them this way and that.

"Feet sore?" Jordan asked me.

I nodded, rolling my eyes. "Poor choice in footwear last night."

She glanced down at my newly acquired shoes. "Good brand. New?"

"Yeah, I splurged today."

"Worth it," she gestured to her own feet. "They're all I ever wear."

That was the end of our lunch conversation.

As we neared the end of our workload, I found myself growing nervous. That was silly, I admonished myself. Just because Dominic singled me out to come work with him, did not mean he thought about me, at all.

With the last cart finished, I pushed it to the door and followed Jordan into the back room. Though I'd been through here on the tour, I was at a loss among the towering shelves.

"This is where all the extras go," Jordan was explaining. "We call it backstock."

"Stock that goes back," I murmured aloud. "Makes sense."

She grinned at me. "You'll be down here, this is the freezer," her hand touched a large, silver door. A second identical door loomed up. "This is dairy."

Farther down, there was a double door that led into a room that was degrees cooler than the back room. There was a tiled floor, pallets lined against the right side with boxes of potatoes and bananas piled high, a double sink and several clipboards hanging along the walls. To the left were two more silver doors, identical to the freezer.

"This is the meat cooler, and this one is produce," Jordan announced, yanking open the first door. Peering through clear plastic strips that hung down just inside the door, Jordan shut the door again before pulling open the second. "He's in here," she gestured for me to enter.

Spreading the plastic pieces aside, I heard Jordan whisper 'have fun' before spinning on her heel to leave. Taking a deep breath, I stepped inside.

Dominic was in there, his presence overwhelming in the small space. The scent of strawberries was overpowering, and the aroma of all the produce mixing together was not altogether pleasant. Holding a small black device in his hand, Dominic turned to face me as I entered. After studying me for a moment, he spoke.

"Welcome to PMDF."

The way he said the word felt as if he were introducing me to my doom. Though it was technically an acronym, standing for produce, meat, dairy and frozen, he pronounced it as one word, 'pimdef.' That had all been explained during orientation, and I was proud of myself for remembering *something* from that day.

"Thanks?" It came out as a question, and I rubbed my exposed arms. Dominic's own arms were bare, and he hardly seemed to notice the chill to the air.

"Cold?" His brows pressed together, glancing at the clear goosebumps I had no hope of warming.

"I wasn't expecting to be in the coolers tonight," I said by way of explanation.

Abandoning the device on the cart he stood next to, Dominic opened the large door for me. "After you."

Stepping out, I remained quiet, not sure what he was up to. From a hook in the main room, he grabbed a jacket and held it out to me. "This is mine, you can borrow it."

"Thanks," I murmured, accepting the clothing. As I pulled my arms through the sleeves, I was immediately enveloped by his scent. It was a mixture of musk and spice that smelled better than any cologne.

He nodded his acknowledgement before heading back into the cooler, allowing me to go first. The sleeves hung well below my fingertips, so I shoved them above my wrists before turning my attention to him.

"So, what would you like me to do?"

"I'll be teaching you how to backstock," he told me. "They have the floor handled for now."

Handing me an extra device, he showed me how to log in and get to the same screen he was on.

"It's a pretty simple process," he told me. "Loose items get placed in these bins, and boxes get placed on the shelves. We have to make sure the older items are placed on top, so when someone comes back here to fill an empty spot, they're not taking the newest stuff."

Nodding along, trying to keep my mind focused on his words when his scent filled my lungs and he stood so close, I didn't fully succeed.

The device I held had a trigger on the bottom, which shot out an infrared light to read barcodes. Dominic had me first scan the item, then the barcode attached to the location it would be placed in. After that, I typed in the quantity and hit enter. Pretty simple, overall, and lucky for me, since my brain had plenty of distraction.

Once he was done explaining, we worked in tandem to finish offloading the carts. We lapsed into silence, and though the tension between us was strong, I also felt oddly at ease. That seemed to be the way with him; constantly filling me with opposing feelings.

We moved on to the meat cooler, and followed the same process. It seemed to me there were easier, more streamlined ways of doing this, but I kept my opinions to myself. I didn't know enough about the entire system to voice my thoughts aloud.

Next, he led me to the dairy cooler. This was a much larger space, and included several shelves of milk and juice that looked extremely heavy. Dominic noticed my stare and grinned at me.

"If you'll handle the open stuff, I'll handle the heavy stuff."

"Deal," I grinned up at him, meeting his eyes.

Something flowed between us, and I felt locked in his gaze once again. How did he *do* that?

He broke the contact first, separating himself from me as much as he was able to in the confined space. I turned to the carts filled with cups of yogurt, cheese packets and smaller bottles of juice. Getting back into the rhythm of scanning, I almost jumped when he spoke.

"Why did you decide to move to Duluth?"

Sneaking one glance at him, I realized his focus was on rearranging the shelves of milk. Clearing my throat, I answered him with my practiced story.

"I came to live with my sister. She needed help with her kids, so I watch them during the day."

Feeling his gaze on me, I looked over at him again. His eyes bore into mine, curiosity brimming, though I couldn't be sure why. It wasn't a very interesting story.

Finally releasing me from his stare, he asked another question. "You said you lived in Tampa, what kind of work did you do there?"

"I worked in a surf shop right on the beach," I told him. I'd timed that to be over the winter, where the unbearably humid weather wouldn't hit me. There were a lot of days I missed walking barefoot in the sand.

"And San Francisco?" Dominic interrupted my short reverie.

"Receptionist in an Engineering firm," I answered him.

"Where else have you lived?" He asked.

"Boston, Savannah, New Orleans, Tucson, Napa Valley, Portland for a little while..."

Trailing off, I turned to see him gawking at me. With a shrug, I continued.

"I also did a study abroad in France, and bounced around Europe just a bit."

"And now you're in Duluth."

"And now I'm in Duluth," I confirmed.

"Because of family."

Nodding, I glanced back at the yogurt in my hand. "Yes. My parents were from around here."

That wasn't true, but it made my move here more plausible.

He grunted in response.

"Where are you from?" I asked, attempting to turn the tables.

"Not here," he said it quietly.

Glancing at him sharply, I coaxed, "Come on, I've told you all kinds of things about me."

It took a few moments, but he gave in. "I was raised in western Iowa."

That was the last thing I had expected.

"Brothers or sisters?" I asked.

"One brother," he told me. "We're very close."

"Did he move here, too? Or is he still back in Iowa?"

He hesitated, just briefly. "Still in Iowa."

Something about that didn't ring true, but I wouldn't begrudge him one inconsistency. I had many.

"What are your parents like?" I asked.

"Dead," he replied starkly.

The finality of the word made me flinch, and my heart reached out to him. Before I could stop myself, I closed the distance between us, laying a hand gently on his forearm. There was a small spark, as if the air was too dry and created static electricity. I didn't let it deter me from touching him.

"I'm so sorry," I told him quietly. Though he wasn't looking directly at me, the sheer sorrow and anger in his eyes had me speaking again, the truth this time, though it wasn't part of my story. "My parents passed away too."

When his eyes met mine again, the curiosity was back, mixing with the other emotions but remaining prevalent. "How old were you?"

Taking my hand back, I looked down. "Young," I answered him. "Too young to remember them clearly, but old enough to experience the pain."

His hand reached out towards me, tentatively, and the pad of his thumb brushed roughly against my cheek. My eyes shot to his again. With his hand cupping my cheek, we stared at one another for an immeasurable amount of time. I felt myself being drawn towards him, and it felt as if the same sensation was affecting him. Our faces came inexorably closer, and my mouth popped open, sucking in air while I had the chance. An odd buzzing of electricity surrounded us. The lights may have flickered, but I was past noticing.

The door pulled open and we jumped apart, both turning our heads towards the intruder, though our bodies remained positioned the same. Luckily, the clear plastic pieces were not completely see through, so even if the person opening the door had looked directly inside, they wouldn't have seen our- almost- compromising position.

"Hey, Dom, you need any help in…"

The man who stood at the door looked familiar, though I hadn't met him yet. He trailed off when he noticed me standing there.

"Oh, I guess not. Where do you want me?"

Dominic regained his composure. Turning abruptly away from me, he walked to the door. "In here. Help Reese finish up, I need to make my rounds."

Without a glance back at me, Dominic walked out of the cooler. I stood, shaking and feeling suddenly, irrationally, bereft. The man turned to me, offering me a smile.

"Cold in here, isn't it?"

Though my shaking had nothing to do with the temperature, I took the out and nodded.

"Yeah," my voice came out cracked. Realizing I still wore Dominic's coat, I wondered how in the world I would work up the nerve to return it to him.

"I'm Kade," he held out a hand to shake.

"Reese," I told him, returning the gesture, my throat still dry.

"I can keep working on the juice, if you want," Kade offered.

"That'd be great, thanks," I told him, turning back to the remains of my cart.

Once I was finished, I helped Kade with the last of the juice and realized it was time for me to go home. Thanking Kade for his help, I peeked out of the door and saw no sign of Dominic, so I snuck back to the room leading to the produce cooler and hung his jacket back on the hook.

With steady steps, I went straight to the locker area, grabbed my things and clocked out, no sign of Dominic on my way.

Bursting into the early morning air, I took a deep breath to calm my frayed nerves. The lot was empty of people, still another hour before the store opened. The sun was already up, peaking through the fog that I was told was normal during the spring. Sometimes it would clear by mid-morning, similar to the effect of the ocean, while other times it would last for days.

The further away from the lake I drove, the less impact the fog had. Though I would have loved to have lived within view of the wide expanse of water, I found the serenity of the little house I'd rented to be perfect. I did make a promise to myself, that each sunny morning, I would drive down to the lake and make use of the paved trail surrounding it.

When I arrived home, little wisps of fog curled around the trunks of trees in the backyard and skittered across the road. Since the moment in the cooler, I'd shut my brain down, refusing to dawdle on what had happened.

Pulling into the driveway and shifting to park, I stared at the tiny house, its happy yellow siding beckoning me inside, but I wasn't ready yet.

Leaving my purse on the seat, I slipped out of the car and headed to the path in the woods. It was dark, gloomy, with a cool breeze, the wind coming off the lake. I began walking, touching the bark of trees as I went, sticking to the well laid path before me. The further I went, the darker the space surrounding me became. Another time, I would have allowed my imagination to run wild, imagining all sorts of creatures stalking through the foliage, but not today.

My walk turned into a run, feet pounding against the dirt, kicking the occasional pine cone out of my way. As I ran, my breath came in quick gasps, my lungs burning for air, but I didn't pause. I ran like there was something chasing me.

Perhaps there was. Not a creature, or even a person, but emotions. New, exciting and terrifying emotions swirled in my chest, beating against my insides, aching to be released. I'd only met Dominic three days ago, and yet he managed to affect me like no else ever had.

He always seemed so aloof towards me, until that one moment in the cooler, the moment that was so rudely interrupted. What would have happened if it had been allowed to continue?

What did I *want* to have happen?

I came to an abrupt halt, hands on my knees, sucking in deep breaths while I faced the truth. Dominic and I had some insane, unbelievable connection, and I wanted him. Not just physically, but all of me wanted all of him. The little quirk of his lips when he was amused made me want to make him laugh. The complete sorrow in his eyes when he spoke of his parents made me want to hear all his darkest secrets.

This shouldn't be happening. This notion that floated through my mind and I refused to put words to. No one could know the things somewhere, deep down, I knew.

Love at first sight wasn't real.

Except, that's exactly how I felt.

My slow walk back through the forest was a blur, just as my run had been. I saw nothing of the scenery surrounding me, didn't hear the chatter of squirrels or the chirp of birds. With my emotions running amuck, I needed to reel them in, and figure out exactly why that was happening. Was it Dominic? Was it the concept of my latest novel? Or was it this city, with its mysterious fog and ever encroaching forest?

The truth was, I didn't know. What I did know, was that I needed to get back on track.

Determination set on my face, I hurried my steps, though I didn't run again. Making it back to the driveway, I scooped my things out of the front seat and went inside the house. Before anything else, I sat down at my computer and began to write, the words flowing out of me like I'd never felt before. I'd unleashed a torrent of emotion, and, as I re-read my words hours later, I knew I'd tapped into something that had been missing. If that was because of Dominic, I'd take it without question.

Feeling better, I took a hot shower then climbed into bed, relishing in the fact that I had three days to focus on my real work, and forget about Dominic.

CHAPTER 5

In the woods again, except this time it was day. Dappled sunlight graced the forest floor as it filtered through the canopy of trees.

This area was unfamiliar, but beautiful just the same. It seemed an endless collection of trees, and as I loped easily through the underbrush, I realized I was not on a path. That didn't seem to hinder my progress at all.

There was a joy in running that I'd never felt before, a freedom in the wind whipping through my hair.

No, not hair.

When I came to a stop, I reached out with an arm to feel the soft ferns springing up, a testament to the season.

Instead of a hand, there was a giant, gray paw.

My days off were productive, putting words to page in a flurry. Several meals were skipped, but I didn't notice. I did manage to keep to my unorthodox schedule, working through the night and sleeping my days away.

By the time I headed back to Wilson's, I had managed to downplay the moment in the cooler as nothing more than a shared moment of painful remembrance.

There was another conclusion I'd come to, and it hadn't been easy. Dominic was a distraction, and I couldn't allow him to deter me from my main purpose. So, I was going to ignore the flutters of excitement when he was in the same room. If he asked a question, I would answer only what he needed to know. And, if we were left in an enclosed space together, I would come up with some reason to leave.

Ignoring him, avoiding the onslaught of emotions that had almost overpowered me, was for the best.

With that new attitude, I walked in through the side door, ready to start work. By that, I meant more than schlepping heavy boxes and rotating expired food. I meant, observing the people I worked with, making new friends, getting a feel for the personalities and overall thoughts of the overnight worker, and completely dismissing any notion of *love at first sight*.

Jacob was behind the desk, greeting me with his typical 'good morning' when I walked in.

With a wide grin, I shot back "Hi, Jake!"

If he was surprised by my bright countenance, he hid it well.

Shoving my purse into a locker, I clocked in then checked the handwritten schedule to see where I would be. First, I looked at the main group, that I had been a part of my first night. When my name wasn't there, I looked to softlines with a hopeful expression. I wasn't there either.

Then, under PMDF, my name was printed in neat block letters.

With a sigh, I spun to the desk to ask Jacob if I could run back out to my car, since I had a jacket out there.

"Sure," he said with a grin. "Hurry back."

With a wry smile, I slipped out the door and jogged to my car, glad I had thought to leave a jacket inside. Though, if working in the coolers would be a more permanent thing, I would have to stock up on hats and gloves, too.

Reaching out for the door, I was beat to it by another hand. Looking up, I smiled in surprise.

"Hi, Kade," I said.

"How's it going?" He asked genially while he held open the door for me.

"Not too bad," I returned, gesturing with the jacket in my hands. "Just getting ready for some fun."

"Cool, I'll be back there too," he told me.

"Actually, Kade, would you mind training Reese in?" Jacob had been eavesdropping on us.

"Sure thing," Kade replied, clocking in and turning towards me. "Ready?"

"As I'll ever be."

Kade led me to the back. There was one other person already in the tiled room that led to the produce and meat coolers, pulling on a giant blue suit that reminded me of a car mechanic. When we walked in, Kade introduced me.

"Reese, Jesse," he said simply.

"Nice to meet you," I said, giving the man with a long, scruffy beard a handshake. He reminded me of a lumberjack, a good head taller than me, shaggy brown hair that matched the beard and a good natured, round face. If he was wearing a plaid shirt under the suit, I may just lose it.

"You, too! They tricked you into working back here, did they?"

"Not sure I had much choice," I grinned. The bear of a man was easy to like.

47

"It's not so bad. They mostly leave us alone, and gets us out of the heavy lifting. Just have to put up with a little cold, but that's not much different than being outside, is it?"

He laughed to himself, turning to Kade. "I'll take the freezer while you show her the ropes."

"Awesome," Kade smiled. "That's my least favorite part."

I had a feeling it would be my least favorite, too.

Tucking a beanie over his mass of hair, Jesse saluted us before sauntering off.

"So, how much did you learn the other night?"

"Not much," I told him, my pulse skittering as my thoughts went unwittingly to the dairy cooler. "Just how to backstock."

Kade nodded. "Let's start with a tour then, shall we? This is the prep room," he spread his arms wide. "It's a little bit cooler in here, so it's a good place to sort the food before either bringing it to the floor or sticking it in the cooler. Things that should be kept at room temperature- potatoes, onions, bananas, that sort of thing- are kept on pallets out here."

His toe nudged the pallet closest to us.

"Back here are some sinks, and the label machine for meat. Not everything has to be weighed by us, and it's used mostly when something is on sale and we have to re-label. These things are used to date the bakery items, and under here are most things you can think of. Markers for the boxes, pens, stickers for various things," he was digging around in the cabinet beneath the sink, showing me examples of everything he listed.

I nodded along, doing my best to remember everything he was telling me.

"You're familiar with the coolers, but let's start in the produce." After grabbing two scanners, he pulled open the big silver door, letting me go inside first. "The first thing we do is bring out food from back here to fill in what's empty on the floor. We call that 'pulling.' The computer does all this for us, so after you log in, you select that option, then find the produce batch."

Watching the screen, I stopped when I saw 'Pro' and showed it to Kade. "This is it?"

"That's it. Hit enter, and it'll tell you which location to scan first."

After scanning the location barcode, I looked back at the screen. It had a description of the item, and how many it wanted me to take.

"Type in how many you're taking, hopefully the full amount its asking for, and hit enter."

Kade helpfully loaded an empty cart while I worked the scanner.

"This is the opposite of backstocking," I said with sudden insight.

"That's right," Kade said approvingly. "Seem pretty easy?"

"Yeah, I think I can handle this."

"Great, I'm going to head into the dairy cooler, it's usually bigger than produce and meat put together. Once you're done, you can try the meat cooler next, and if you need me just come grab me from dairy."

"Sounds good," I told him, focusing back on my scanning.

Once I was alone, I pulled out my earbuds, hooked them into my phone and pressed play on my book, picking up from where I left off three nights ago. Hanging out in the cooler was certainly more enjoyable than I'd originally thought it would be.

It didn't take long to get done in the produce, and I noticed with annoyance that more than once, the system had me grabbing an item from a bin, leaving others of the same, only to have me taking one or two items out of a box later down the line. Obviously, the system wasn't perfect, and once again, I found myself wondering if there was a better way of doing this.

Leaving the full cart in the cooler, I headed next to the meat cooler. Scrolling through the scanner, I found the batch listed as 'Mea,' and got to work.

From a few stints in restaurants, I knew there was a specific order to stack the raw meat as I loaded it into the cart. I was careful to keep the chicken on the bottom, and the deli meat on top. As I was nearing the end of the batch, the door popped open and Kade stuck his head in.

"Oh, hey, I forgot to tell you about stacking the meat..." He trailed off, examining the cart as I had it. "Never mind, you got it. Did you know that already?"

"I've worked in restaurants," I told him. "I figured it was the same here."

"Nice job. You almost done?"

Nodding, I scanned the last location. "That's it."

"Cool, I'm done in the dairy, so we'll stick together for the next part."

Nodding, I followed him out of the cooler, pushing out one of the carts while Kade took the other. "Anything in PMDF can only be on the floor for 30 minutes, so we don't bring out too much at once."

"Got it," I assured him.

"Where you from?" He asked as we walked.

50

"I've lived all over," I told him truthfully.

"Oh, yeah? What was your favorite place?"

Before I answered, I thought about that. "Every place I've been, I've found something to love about it. But, I'd have to say, my favorite overall city was Savannah. It had so much history, it was right on the water, and even though it was a large enough city to have the stores I liked, it still had a small-town feel. Lots of little festivals, celebrating the most random things."

"That's awesome."

"Are you from Duluth?" I asked him.

"Born and raised. But, I like it."

"It seems like a fun town, and lots of outdoorsy stuff."

"Have you been here over a winter yet?"

Shaking my head, I brought my cart to a halt next to his. "I'm not sure how I'd fare. I've heard horror stories."

"It can get bad, but it's not *always* bad. About one year in five will be extra cold, and temperatures will be something like negative 40-60, for weeks straight."

I shivered in response. "That sounds horrible."

"Other years we'll get a ton of snow, I've seen it drop three or four feet in a night."

"How do you even deal with that?" I asked, shocked.

He shrugged. "When you grow up with it, it's not such a big deal. Schools might shut down for that, but otherwise we just keep going to work like normal."

Shaking my head in wonder, I began checking the expiration dates of the product I was putting out. Breaking from our conversation to show me how many of each item could be stacked and how high, Kade went right back to asking me questions.

"Why did you decide to move here?"

"My sister lives here," I told him. "I've got a niece and a nephew that I help watch during the day."

The rest of the night continued like this, and I found myself enjoying conversation with Kade. He was a few years younger than me, and going to school to be a graphics designer. Though we really had nothing in common, he was very easy to talk with, and I found myself opening up to him, as much as I was able to, anyway. The night went by quickly, and my thoughts hardly strayed toward Dominic at all.

At our first break, I realized Jordan wasn't here, but I decided to sit at the table we'd used before. I knew, once I got to know more people and felt more comfortable around them, that sitting in the break room would become easier.

I spent the break happily entranced by the e-book I'd been reading, checking the time and realizing I was late for the nightly meeting. Rushing inside, I halted just outside the doorway, and peered inside.

The managers had just stood up, rattling off the numbers, which I'd come to realize were regarding the truck size, and how much had gone to each area of the store.

My eyes unerringly found the man I'd been successfully avoiding all night. He leaned against the counter, scanning the group as was his habit. When they landed on me, he quickly looked towards the opposite side of the room. I was momentarily crushed, before I remembered I was the one who had pushed him away.

He didn't know that, though, a tiny voice reminded me.

You can't have it both ways! I argued back.

Great, I was arguing with myself, even if only inside my head. Worse than that, I was losing.

It would help if he didn't look so sexy, wearing the tight, worn in jeans he was fond of or the dark blue t-shirt that stretched across his chest and strained against his biceps. Before I could help myself, my eyes drifted down again, to his tattoos. I still wondered what the symbols could be.

When we were dismissed, my eyes flicked back up to his face for just a moment, and he was watching me. Jumping back with a start, I spun on my heel and walked away. I didn't even care it was the long way around to the coolers.

CHAPTER 6

Kade, Jesse and I finished with our work just after lunch, so we joined the rest of the team to help them finish. Kade had told me a fresh food truck came in three times a week, and those nights were hectic. Though no one had said as much, I was assuming I would be part of the team for PMDF. Part of me wondered if that meant more time alone with Dominic. If tonight was any indication, where it had felt like he'd avoided me like the plague, I thought, perhaps, not.

A couple of hours before I was set to go home, Jacob found me.

"Would you mind helping Gabi over in cosmetics?"

With a shrug, I agreed.

When I reached the cosmetic section, I took one look at the carts filled with tiny little boxes and my eyes widened.

"Hi!" A girl with dark brown hair, hazel eyes and a pair of glasses that managed to look stylish instead of nerdy greeted me, drawing out the single word longer than was necessary.

"Hey," I greeted her. "I'm Reese, Jacob sent me to help."

"Oh, *good*, there's *so* much tonight!"

I found myself liking Gabi immediately, much the same as Jesse. She stressed most of her words, giving her a Valley girl personality. It was readily apparent that drama, not necessarily in a bad way, followed her around.

"Anything special I need to know?" I asked her.

"Yes! Put all the little boxes into a big box when they're empty, they'll be *so* much easier to crush then."

"Got it," I grinned, and set to work.

We were in the same aisle, and she talked nonstop. It was highly entertaining, and I found myself laughing constantly.

"So," she sidled up close to me, dropping her voice to a whisper. "Who would you do?"

Choking out a laugh, I spluttered, "What?"

Her eyes widened. "You've never played who would you do? Oh my gosh, it's so much fun. Whenever I go out with my girlfriends, we have to pick one person in the room we'd hook up with."

"Oh," I answered her, looking around wildly. "I'm... I'm not sure."

Liar. There was just no way I was admitting the truth to this talkative girl.

"Seriously? Me, I pick Jake."

"The manager?" I verified.

"Yes! Isn't he adorable?"

Glancing around, checking to see if anyone was near us, I gave her a noncommittal answer. "Sure."

"Come on, you have to tell me. Of everyone here tonight, who would you pick?"

"Um..."

Before I could answer, I felt the hairs on my arm stand up. With a groan, I turned, knowing who was approaching the aisle.

Gabi turned too, with eyes as wide as mine had just been as Dominic appeared from around the corner.

"Dominic! How *are* you?"

"Fine, how are you ladies?" He answered.

"Good! Reese is blowing through these boxes, so we'll be done in *no* time!"

"Great." With that, he turned and walked away.

Letting out a breath, I concentrated on the mascara in my hand, matching the color to the correct peg.

"I wouldn't kick him out of bed for eating crackers," Gabi commented as she joined me.

Another choking laugh came out. "Where do you come up with this stuff?"

Her eyes settled on me, wide and innocent. "Are you telling me you don't think he's hot?"

"I... uh, well, I hadn't noticed."

She snorted gracefully. "Yeah, right. He's super-hot, and you know it. I don't know, though, I think I'd still pick Jake. Dominic seems mean, and controlling. I like to have control, if you know what I mean. Jake seems like a little puppy dog, perfect for me to train."

Seeming lost in her own thoughts, I didn't respond to Gabi. Even if she had been expecting a response, I wasn't sure what I would have said to any of that. I wasn't used to someone being so nonchalant about their love interests.

The next night at work, I was back in the PMDF department. Kade wasn't there tonight, though Jesse was, along with another man named Ricky. Ricky was older, and quiet, walking with a stoop that predicated lifelong physical work. He didn't say much to me, but Jesse made up for it by joking with me and offering to show me the freezer.

Pulling on one of the jumpsuits that were offered, I donned my jacket, gloves and hat that I'd luckily remembered to bring, and prepared to enter the freezing space.

It was even worse than I'd imagined. Life on the beach had not prepared me for such bitter cold.

Having Jesse with me took my mind off it, just slightly, and since we were both working in the same batch, it was half the time one of us would have been in there alone.

The cold quickly seeped through all my layers, but my thin cotton gloves I'd purchased for a dollar were by far the worst offenders. I learned to grab bags of vegetables by the edges, as touching just the plastic was less severe than grabbing the frozen chunks in between.

Once we stepped back into the hallway, Jesse clapped my back as I shivered uncontrollably.

"How do you *do* that, every night?" I asked, bewildered, trying without avail to warm my fingers by blowing into my hands.

"That's nothing. Wait until one of our winters, it will feel warm in there in comparison."

My face paled at the thought. As I began walking towards the prep room to remove the extra layers of clothes, my shoes made an odd noise on the floor. I glanced down, miffed.

"I think even my shoes are frozen," I grumbled to Jesse.

He let out a booming laugh. "Yeah, some soles will do that. Give them a few minutes, they'll thaw out."

"Is there anywhere still selling winter boots?" I asked, not completely joking.

Jesse laughed again, slapping me on the back lightly, but hard enough to force me to take a step forward to catch my balance.

"You're a funny one!"

Peeling the jumpsuit off, I put the jacket back on, along with the gloves, little help though they were.

Jesse watched me, still shivering, and spoke again. "Why don't you bring some of the carts to the floor? Ricky and I can finish up in the coolers."

With a grateful smile, I nodded at that, heading back to the cursed freezer. Managing to yank a cart out, I walked slowly with it to the floor, my frozen shoes echoing along the concrete as if I were wearing heels. The backroom where the truck had been unloaded was now empty. As another shiver racked my body, I couldn't help but wonder what I had gotten myself into.

Walking past the main group and heading towards the freezer, I was surprised to hear my name called out.

"Reese!"

Turning, I found the source and smiled in greeting. "Hey, Gabi!"

She bounced over to me, eyes bright. "You're working in PMDF? I wouldn't mind being there, but the freezer is *so cold*. How do you handle it?"

"Not very well," I laughed. "Luckily, Jesse helped me out, otherwise someone probably would have found me frozen solid on the floor."

She laughed and waved as she headed back to the aisle she was working.

The smile from our brief interaction stayed on my lips. At least *someone* here liked me.

That wasn't fair, I reminded myself. Plenty of people had been nice, and friendly. There was just the one glaring exception.

Putting him out of my mind, I braced myself to open the cooler doors to begin putting the frozen food away. It was almost as bad as being in the cooler, except I could still feel my legs. Hurrying as much as I was able, I sagged with relief when I spotted Jesse wheeling out the other cart from the freezer. That meant I could work on something just a *bit* warmer.

Jordan was back at the table during the first break, and I sat silently across from her as we had before.

"Where are you tonight?" She asked, though the jacket I was still wearing should have been a giveaway.

"PMDF," I told her. "Jesse made me go in the freezer."

She laughed at my predicament good naturedly. "I told them I'd be willing to be a backup for that, so maybe we'll get to work together again one day."

"That's be awesome," I grinned at her.

When we approached the breakroom for the meeting, Gabi spotted me and waved from across the room. Giving her a shy wave back, I glanced up to the managers and met the eyes I'd been doing my best not to think about. He didn't look away as quickly as he had the night before, and I searched his face for some clue as to what he wanted. When he finally turned away, I had the strangest feeling that we both felt unsatisfied.

It was a quick night for PMDF, and I found myself back with the main group before lunch. As 3:00 hit, Gabi found me.

"You should come sit with me for lunch!" She said, gripping my forearm lightly.

"All right," I found myself agreeing. Her strong personality was difficult to object to.

First grabbing my salad from one of the fridges, I sat beside Gabi, taking a long pull on my water bottle. There were two others sitting at the same table, and to my surprise, Becca was one of them.

Gabi began talking immediately, and didn't stop until break was over. There was very little I had to contribute, which I was thankful for, and it helped pass the time, keeping my mind off both the horrible smells and *him*.

"I ran into Jake this morning," Gabi's voice had dropped into a whisper.

"Really? Where?"

"At a *bar*," she told me.

Though this sounded strange out of context, I realized that, as an overnight worker, the morning time was after work, and many people went out drinking. When thinking about it like that, drinking at night was actually stranger.

"Was it weird?" I asked.

"*No*," she giggled. "We just sat and talked for *hours*."

"That's... nice," I finished unenthusiastically.

As we got up to leave the breakroom, I noticed Dominic hadn't been in the room, and I wondered briefly where he could be. Only briefly, though.

The rest of the night went by easily, and as I was leaving I found myself saying goodbye to people, calling them by name. It was a good feeling.

When I got home, I collapsed happily into bed.

The forest was different. Instead of towering evergreens and thick underbrush as I was becoming used to, the variety of oak and maple left the ground free to traverse. The air was crisp with autumn, the leaves a brilliant cornucopia of color even in the fading light. There was no fear in me as I stretched my limbs, leaping over the rocky terrain of Pike's Peak State Park.

I wasn't alone. Another presence shared my joy as we loosely raced toward the waterfall, splashing in the shallow water, shooting large sprays up and biting into them with our strong jaws.

Once again, I was the gray wolf. Beside me, a great red-brown wolf leapt up, landing sideways to create a wave that washed over me.

Shaking off the excess, I sprang towards him, ready to settle the score.

The next two nights I had no work, though I had plenty to catch up on with Sydney. Her vampire didn't avoid her like my almost-interest did, and I felt slightly envious of the character I had created.

To break up the tedium, I drove down to the lake walk each morning I had off, wanting to watch the sunrise over the mass of blue. Since I was staying up all night, it wasn't a difficult task to meet the dawn.

Though I enjoyed being right on the water, I also found some gorgeous trails higher up the hill. One particular winding road boasted cliff edges with stunning views of the lake, the bridges Duluth was famous for, and across the bay, Superior laid out in a contrarily flat combination of buildings and greenery.

There was definitely more than met the eye here. I wondered if Sydney would see that too, and come to a new appreciate of her hometown.

CHAPTER 7

Working overnights slowly became a routine, by far the strangest routine I'd ever had, but a routine nonetheless. Gabi and I spent each break together, giggling like teenagers most of the time. It was rare for me to click so easily with someone, and I enjoyed her company.

When she wasn't around, I sat with Jordan, who was slowly opening up to me. Her sarcastic humor never failed to both make me laugh and feel inadequate, barely being able to keep up with her quick thoughts. Occasionally, Gabi and Jordan would both sit with me, but they didn't seem to click together as well as I had with each of them separately.

Most nights I was in the PMDF department, and even though I still had trouble for long periods in the freezer, I was getting surprisingly used to the cold. I'd been scheduled for each night we'd received a truck, and Kade had been right in his initial assessment. Those nights were hectic.

"What are you reading?"

I glanced over at Kade with a grin. Earlier, when I was alone in the coolers and could talk to myself without being questioned, I'd been learning Italian. Now, I was back to a favorite. "Count of Monte Cristo."

He rolled his eyes back at me. "Again? You were listening to that when we first met."

Ripping open another box of yogurt, I answered him, "That's because it's a good story. True love, the kind they don't make anymore. Plus, the whole revenge thing."

"I guess," he muttered. "So, what's the latest?"

Laughing to myself, I put more canisters on the shelf. Somehow, in the few short weeks I'd been working in PMDF, Kade and I had developed an unlikely friendship, based on the fact that I relayed gossip to him. Of course, the only reason I had any gossip to relay was because of Gabi.

"Not much since yesterday, Kade." Checking my watch, I added, "Five until break."

We both grabbed a cart filled with food and began pushing them back to the cooler.

"Come on, there has to be *something*," he pressed. "What about Gabi and…"

Before he could say the name, I slapped his arm lightly. Looking pointedly towards a group of people we passed, I raised a brow as a reminder. Gabi's relationship, for however long this one lasted, was very hush-hush. This was her third boyfriend in as many weeks as I'd known her. If I was ever looking for the definition of boy crazy, I was sure Gabi's picture would suffice.

I remembered, very clearly, Gabi's assertions about Jacob the first night I'd met her. Far as I knew, managers were not supposed to date other employees, but Jacob had bent the rules for Gabi.

"You know he can get in trouble," I hissed. We made our way to the backroom and were momentarily away from the crowds.

Kade jumped on the chance. "So?"

"Last I knew, they're fighting again. Something about a drunken text and cats."

"That guy drinks a lot," he responded. "Wait, cats?"

Laughing, I replied, "Yeah, it seems he does. I don't know, something about him wanting to get a cat with her? Anyway, they'll probably be made up by break time."

"Way too soon to talk about joint animal ownership," Kade mumbled.

Just then, the announcement for break sounded overhead. Kade and I walked towards the main part of the store together.

"Reese!" I heard my name squealed from the left.

"See ya," Kade muttered before hunting up something to eat.

"Hey, Gabi," I greeted as she bounded over, coming to a halt next to my side. It still amazed me how quickly we'd become attached, and how easy it was to lapse into giggly teenage girl mode when we were together. "What's up?"

She rolled her eyes. "J's being a moron, but what's new?"

Nodding soberly, I asked, "Still fighting?"

"Well, he's out drinking, *again*, and I'm getting texts between 'I love you' and 'I'll never dress my cat in sweaters.'"

Raising my brows, I asked, "Is this a cat he already has, or the one he wants to get with you?"

"He doesn't have a cat! That's what makes all of this so crazy! What am I supposed to *do* with that?"

We entered the breakroom together, taking our usual seats. Now that I had someone to distract me, I hardly noticed the smells wafting from the microwaves.

Shaking my head, slightly baffled myself, I finally responded to Gabi. "You should write him a message that says you'd rather talk to him tomorrow, when he's sober, and then stop responding."

"Yeah, you're right," Gabi sighed, though we both knew she wouldn't follow my advice. She looked up, then leaned closer to me. "Speaking of forbidden fruit…"

Automatically, I glanced up, then reprimanded myself. Other than very brief, very polite work-related conversations, I hadn't spoken to Dominic. Or thought about him. Much.

Somewhere in our conversations, Gabi had uncovered the truth about my feelings towards him, in that I had some kind of crazy attraction to him. She also knew I didn't want to get involved, but that didn't stop her from teasing me about it at every turn.

Noah, Becca and Jesse took their usual seats across from us. Noah and Jesse were always easy to talk with, and we'd eventually broken Becca out of her shell. She still had the same glaring attitude towards everyone else, but at least at our lunch table, she would crack a smile every now and again.

"We should go out tonight," Gabi interrupted my thoughts. "We both have it off, it would be fun!"

Though I wasn't much of a partier, I thought a night out, with actual people, might do me some good.

"I'm in," I told her. Glancing across the table, I asked, "What about you guys?"

"Working," Noah said glumly.

"Me, too," Becca added.

"Not a drinker," Jesse grinned at us. "But have fun."

Turning back to Gabi, I asked, "Where should we meet? Or, I can come pick you up, so we can drive together."

"That would be awesome!" She gushed, and I was happy for my decision. As well as I'd gotten to know Gabi, I was sure she'd be in no condition to drive home.

I found Gabi's apartment with a little help from my map app, heading towards the door when she told me she wasn't ready yet. She greeted me mostly dressed, with half her dark hair piled on top of her head and the other half hanging in loose curls. She had forgone her glasses tonight, and though it wasn't the first time I'd seen her in contacts, it was always a small shock at the way it changed her face.

"Come talk to me while I get ready!" She exclaimed, pulling me along through a tiny living room. A galley kitchen was on the left, her bathroom on the right, and her bedroom was straight ahead. Not much space, but perfect for a single person.

69

"Cute place," I told her, looking around at the completely random decorating that somehow managed to fit her personality to a T.

The living room had a loveseat that was bright red, a side chair that was turquoise blue and an old barrel that was used as a table. Hanging on the walls were brightly colored canvases, art prints of cats and motivational sayings splashed in glitter. Personally, I'd never be able to pull it off, but I found myself really enjoying the eclectic taste.

"Thanks!" She responded, standing at the sink.

"Can I help?" I asked, but Gabi shook her head.

"Jacob and I are done," she announced, yanking out the clips holding the top of her hair in place. As she began to run chunks through an iron, she continued, "I told him just a little while ago. That's why I'm running late."

"Oh, I'm so sorry," I told her. "How did he take it?"

She shrugged. "Not too good. He's got to work tonight, though, so at least I know he won't be out drinking."

Nodding in agreement, I fiddled with some lipstick lying on her counter. "That's too bad, though."

"Yeah," she sighed. "He was a nice guy, but he got so *clingy*. Not for me."

"So, we're looking for a rebound tonight?" I asked.

"Oh, no! We're looking for *you*."

"Me?" I squeaked. "No, I'm good."

Gabi rolled her eyes, leaned closer to the mirror to inspect her eyelashes before releasing the portion of hair and collecting another. "You are so *not* good, you just have no idea."

Moving my shoulders restlessly, I attempted to explain. "I'm not attracted easily."

"That's just because you don't give anyone a chance. Tell me, honestly, when was the last time you opened yourself up to a relationship? Or even just a good time?"

My thoughts flickered to Dominic, but I immediately reeled myself in. "It's hard to explain. When I meet someone, it's like I know, right off, if it could lead somewhere."

"How do you really know, though, if you don't give them a chance?" She pressed.

"I've never been wrong," I defended. "Plus, it's not like I'm mean to guys. I still get to know them, and like them as friends. There's just never anything more there."

Watching me through the mirror, Gabi grabbed the last chunk of hair before speaking again. "I think you're just waiting for the right one."

"Yeah," I agreed, hoping it would close the discussion.

"But, that doesn't mean you shouldn't have fun in the meantime," she punctuated this by pointing the end of the curling iron at me. Clicking the button to off, she spun towards me. "I'm ready, let's go!"

Gabi lived in downtown Duluth, and she directed me towards a bar even further east. At this point, I was about half an hour from my house, and in uncharted territory.

For a small city, Duluth certainly had a lot of neighborhoods to get lost in.

Pulling into the lot of an old hotel, I was happy to find we were right on the lake. Gabi dragged me inside and up several flights of stairs until we found two stools in a martini bar. It was fancier than anything I'd given Duluth credit for.

There was a DJ in an adjoining room, left open as a dancefloor. The beat pounded into my brain, making it difficult to have a conversation.

"So," Gabi shouted into my ear. "Who would you do?"

Laughing, used to her off the wall questions now, I took a slow perusal around the room. I knew, even if I chose someone, nothing would happen. Sometimes, it was just easier to play along.

"By the door, black button down," I yelled back.

Gabi's eyes shot to my target and gave me an incredulous look. "Really? *That's* your type?"

Giving my choice another look, I shrugged in Gabi's direction. The man was short, with a slightly stocky build. Though his clothes were dressy, he wore converse on his feet. He looked absolutely uncomfortable, and that, I could understand completely.

"Let's go talk to him!" Gabi made a grab for my hand.

Quicker than she was, I pulled back, gesturing towards the bar. "Why don't we get a drink first?"

"Okay!" Gabi was easily diverted.

Sighing with relief, I ordered us each a chocolate martini- though I didn't usually drink, I couldn't imagine anything chocolate flavored would be too horrible to sip on for the night.

Once our drinks were set before us, Gabi did a search of her own. "Oh, he's cute!"

Glancing to where her attention had been drawn, I found a group of men looking barely old enough to be in here. They were the preppy type, and I had them pegged for college aged. At this time of year, if they weren't already done with school, they would be soon.

One looked our way, and Gabi gave him a little wave. Swiveling my head back to her, I raised a brow. "They look a little young for us."

"More stamina," Gabi grinned back with a wink. "I think he's coming over here."

"Ladies," the one who had scoped us out leaned against the counter, right between the two of us, his back to me.

Leaning away, a bit peeved at the intrusion, I attempted to crane my neck around him to get Gabi's attention. Unfortunately, she was completely falling for whatever line he'd used.

I sat back, arms crossed, annoyance on my face. It was one thing to be ignored by some arrogant jerk, it was another to be forgotten by the person I'd driven here, who was supposed to be my friend.

Scooting back so my face wasn't shoved into his back, I turned to the bar and took a sip of the drink. It went down smooth, and reminded me of a melted chocolate shake.

After a few minutes, Gabi stood, her hand wrapped in Jerky McJerkerson's.

"We're going to dance!" She shouted towards me. "You should come, too!"

"I'm good," I told her, still irritated.

It didn't seem to affect Gabi, and she dragged the willing guy to the dancefloor. Sitting alone at the bar was not exactly my idea of a good time, and not what I had expected of tonight.

With nothing else to do, I drained my glass more quickly than I had planned. Since Gabi's drink was sitting untouched on the bar, I started in on hers next. They were still dancing when I had two empty glasses sitting before me.

The bartender came over, with a raised brow and a gesture between the glasses. Giving him a thumbs up, I swiveled in my chair, taking another good look around the room. Suddenly, the hairs on my arms stood at attention, and I found myself searching the shadows of the dimly lit room. Only one person gave me that kind of reaction.

Shaking my head at my silliness, I turned back to the bar to find two more martinis waiting for me. With a shrug, I grabbed them both and stood up.

My head did a slow spin, not entirely unpleasant. Stopping at the doorway between the bar and the dancefloor, I saw Gabi happily in Jerky's arms. I tried to get her attention, but to no avail. With another shrug and a long sip, I turned and headed towards the patio area I'd spied in my searching. Some fresh air was exactly what I needed.

CHAPTER 8

There were less people out here, for which I was grateful, and I found a seat right along the railing easily. Setting one empty glass down, I took another long pull on the second. Why had I always been against alcohol? This was delicious.

"Oh, look at the boats!" I slurred, half standing to lean over the rail. In my slightly drunken state, there was an accent on my 'O's' that sounded suspiciously like a character from *Fargo*.

"Those aren't boats, those are *ships*," a helpful voice corrected me from my right.

"What's the difference?" I asked, curious. The man with the voice was with one other friend, both drinking martinis.

"Boats are on a lake. Ships can go on the ocean."

"That's so cool!" I exclaimed, feeling a bit like Gabi.

The man turned towards me more, happy to impart knowledge. "We call them *salties*," he informed me. "They've come through the canals all the way from the Atlantic Ocean."

"Holy crap," I told him, all vestiges of proper grammar forgotten. Another sip drained my glass.

He smiled, understanding the alcohol in my system but choosing to ignore it. "Did you know everything out there," he gestured widely, encompassing the main part of the lake, "is considered International waters?"

My jaw dropped. "Does that mean we could get married on a ship out there?"

He laughed heartily. "I guess so, if you found a willing captain. And could get out there."

Lurching out of my chair, I sat heavily next to my new friends. "I've got a great idea! We'll swim out there, and get married! All three of us. That's legal on International waters, right?"

"You will do no such thing," a hard voice interrupted my brilliant planning.

There was a reason the goosebumps had never disappeared, I'd just stopped caring, thanks to the martinis and my new friends.

"Dominic!" I called out happily. "These are my friends! Hey, guys, what are your names?"

Both men at the table laughed, then immediately silenced when they got a good look at Dominic's thunderous face.

"Oh, uh, it was nice to meet you," one stammered as they both stumbled to their feet, in such a rush to leave the patio they forgot their drinks.

Frowning up at Dominic, I asked, "Why did they leave?"

He yanked me up by my arm, and my back was instantly against the railing. His body was pressed into mine, and I had a wild thought that it felt as if it was built for me.

"What do you think you're doing?" He growled.

Eyebrows drawing down, I gestured towards the now empty glasses left on the table. "Having a drink," I told him as if it was obvious. Dimly, I noticed the rest of the patio had cleared.

"I can see that," his voice was so deep, so rough, I lifted my fingers to his cheek to try to smooth out the hard look.

"What are you doing here?" I asked, my head still spinning. Though I was slow at connecting dots, my body hadn't forgotten for a moment that he was pressed up against me. It was a good thing, too, because I wasn't sure I could stand on my own.

He bit off a curse, pacing away from me. My hands managed to catch against the railing in time, and I took the moment to come to grips as I shivered once from losing his warmth.

"Sit down before you fall down," he snarled at me.

Finally, his mood had filtered through my alcohol soaked mind.

"What's your problem?" I spoke louder now, more harshly. "It's none of your business if I want to go out and have a drink!"

"It is when you're making a fool of yourself!"

Looking around, realizing again that the patio had been deserted, I responded, "By talking to people? I have every right to talk to whomever I please. You have no say over me, or my life."

"Don't remind me," he said under his breath, though I couldn't be sure that's what I heard, as it made no sense.

"I think you should leave," I managed to stand straight, giving my request a little boost.

He spun towards me again, stalking forward. His dark countenance made me swallow in alarm.

His hands grasped the railing on either side of my body, effectively trapping me. Though no part of him touched me, I could feel my body screaming to be in his embrace.

As his face inched closer to mine, my breath came out in quick gasps. I couldn't tell if he was going to kiss me or strangle me, and I couldn't manage to make myself care, as long as contact was made.

"Reese!" Gabi's voice broke through the tense moment. She pushed open the door, then stopped still, her eyes wide.

"Reese needs to leave now," Dominic spoke through gritted teeth, just loud enough for Gabi to hear. He still hadn't shifted from his position. "Are you sober enough to drive her?"

"Sure," Gabi nodded, her bubbly attitude diminished.

Dominic stared down at me, leaning close again. The tension built from anticipation of our earlier moment was gone, but I still reacted to him. "Stay with Gabi tonight. Get home safely in the morning."

Helpless to do anything but nod, Dominic backed away, into the shadows of the corner as he watched us disappear through the patio door.

I woke the next morning with a pounding head and a sore back. Glancing down at what had been my bed for the night, the aching back immediately made sense.

Gabi's loveseat, while over-stuffed and comfortable to sit on, did not make for a good night's sleep.

Sitting up, I looked around groggily, wondering when Gabi would be awake. I could use some coffee and a handful of aspirin.

Stumbling blearily to the bathroom, I washed my face, scrubbing off the extra makeup I'd worn the night before. Hoping Gabi wouldn't mind the intrusion, I took a peak in her cabinet for some kind of medicine. Finding a bottle of Ibuprofen, I praised her name.

In her kitchen, I pulled out a glass and used the tap for water, gulping down four of the pills. As I leaned against the counter, waiting for them to take effect, Gabi popped out of her room.

She wore leopard print pajamas, with a sleep mask shoved up to her forehead. The look did nothing to lessen her beautiful face.

"How do you manage to look like that in the morning?" I groaned.

"Oh, stop, you look fine," she waved a hand. "How's the head?"

"It'll be better soon," I gestured with the bottle, adding, "hope you don't mind."

"Of course not! How much did you drink, anyway?"

"Four martinis? I think, anyway. It probably hit me so hard because one, I never drink, and two, I drank them all in very quick succession."

"That'll do it!" She said, a bit too loudly.

Wincing, I brought a hand to my forehead. "Shh…"

Gabi laughed. "How about some breakfast? There's a place just down the street, we can walk, get you some fresh air."

"Sounds great," I told her. Taking stock of my clothes, I decided they were good enough to wear out in public again.

Gabi got dressed quickly, throwing her hair into a pony and not bothering with makeup. I appreciated that, especially after watching her getting ready to go out the night before. There were too many females out there who had to primp and look perfect before they stepped out of the house, and I would have thought Gabi was one of them. Knowing that food was more important than globs of makeup and hair products had her going up a notch, in my book.

As we began our trek towards the breakfast place, Gabi linked her arm with mine. This normally would have felt silly, but with Gabi, it just felt natural.

"All right, I have to ask," she finally blurted out. "What was going on with you and Dominic last night?"

"I have no idea," I answered truthfully. "Most of the time he just ignores me. He appeared out of nowhere last night, and started ordering me around. I think I yelled at him. That part's a little fuzzy."

Throwing her head back in a laugh, Gabi stopped and pulled open the door to the small diner. We found a table in the back.

"I could have sworn he was about to kiss you," Gabi continued our conversation as soon as we sat.

"Either that or throttle me," I muttered.

"Believe me, if there's one thing I know, it's men," Gabi insisted. "He was going to kiss you. I feel bad about interrupting."

"Don't," I shrugged, playing off my suddenly jittery stomach. "It's a bad idea."

"Those can be the most fun ideas," Gabi winked at me over the menu she was perusing.

"Either way, let's just keep this between us, okay?" I felt I had to state the obvious.

"Of course! You kept my secret about Jake." She rolled her eyes, "Speaking of. Look at how many messages were on my phone this morning."

Tapping a few buttons on her phone's screen, she handed it over. As I scrolled, the messages getting more desperate, I shook my head.

"I'm glad you didn't respond to any of this," I told her.

"Yeah, I'm over it. Plus, I have Tim's number now."

"Would he be the guy from last night?" Jerky McJerkerson, I added silently.

"Yes! He was so cute, and such a good dancer. You should have joined us!"

"I'm not much of a dancer," I told her. That wasn't necessarily true, but explaining to her that I didn't want to be a third wheel seemed arbitrary.

The waiter brought us coffee, and I asked if he would leave us the refill pot. He grinned in understanding, dropping off an extra bowl of creamer along with it. Gabi ordered French toast with eggs; I ordered a stack of pancakes, eggs, bacon and hash browns, with a side of fruit. You know, to stay healthy.

Normally I didn't eat quite so much, but this was like my dinner time, and I needed something to soak up the leftover alcohol still sloshing around my system.

"When do you work next?" Gabi asked me after my third cup of coffee.

With a groan, I told her, "Tonight."

"Me, too! I was thinking I should request to be put in PMDF, so we can work together."

"That would be awesome," I told her, and I thought about Kade. Though he enjoyed the drama, I wasn't sure he appreciated its source.

"What are you going to do when you see Dominic?" Gabi asked, leaning forward in anticipation of my answer.

"Ignore him?" My response came out as a question. "I don't know, what am I supposed to do?"

"Take him into one of the dark corners of the stock room and have your *way* with him," Gabi suggested.

This time I rolled my eyes. "There are cameras everywhere," I reminded her.

"Not in the coolers," she reminded me.

This made me laugh. "Point taken, but it's still a no."

"Fine, how about I set you up with someone instead? Seriously, we need to get you out of this rut."

Our food was delivered then, so I waited a beat to answer. "I'm perfectly happy as is."

She grunted in response, unbelieving. Truth be told, I also had a hard time accepting my words.

CHAPTER 9

When I finally got home, I was too wound up from coffee to sleep, and too hungover to do anything active. Giving my house a halfhearted cleaning, I sat down and attempted to write, but that didn't hold my attention as well as normal, either. Finally, I gave up and went for a drive.

There was still a lot of the area I hadn't explored. When I asked around at work, many people had told me about driving up the North Shore. With that in mind, I made my way through downtown Duluth, to the end of the main highway, and continued onto a scenic route that would drive along the lake. There were several spots to pull off, but I ignored them for now. The sky was a deep blue, as was the water, with the sun shining and no fog to obscure the view. It was also an abnormally warm day, almost hitting 70 degrees.

Laughing to myself, I realized a few months ago, in the dead of winter, Florida had been warmer than that every day.

While I drove, my thoughts went unerringly to Dominic. Though my memory of last night was slightly fuzzy, I couldn't help but question everything that had transpired. First, the fact that he had even been in the same place as Gabi and I was strange. A martini bar didn't really seem like his scene, and it had seemed he was alone.

Then, his anger when he found me speaking with other men- even though, I was relatively certain, they were gay. I hadn't recognized the emotion last night in my martini fog, but he had been jealous.

But why? Why would a man like that, who spent the majority of his time ignoring me, be jealous? It made no sense.

Not least, there was the moment Gabi had interrupted. She thought he was about to kiss me. I had felt the same. And that made even *less* sense.

I had to do something about this, even though the thought of confronting him almost caused a nervous breakdown.

After half an hour of driving the scenic route, I began to see signs for Gooseberry Falls. That piqued my interest, so I followed the directions and eventually wound up at a state park. Trees just beginning to sprout new life surrounded the parking lot, and I took a deep breath of the fresh air as I stepped out of my car. There weren't many other cars in the lot- it was the middle of a weekday, after all- and I was fine with that. A nice relaxing walk was exactly what I needed.

Following the paved path, I found a little dirt trail that was just a small offshoot of the paved one, leading to a single bench. Thinking that odd, I glanced up and took in a swift breath.

Evergreen, oak and various other trees I couldn't name dipped down into a valley spread out before me. A bright blue river cut a path through the green, winding its way to Lake Superior in the distance. The lake sparkled in the sun, fading into the horizon. It looked more like an ocean now than I'd ever seen it.

For a while I just sat on the bench, breathing in the fresh air and finding peace in the quiet of nature. When I finally decided to move along, I continued down the paved path which led past a welcome building, down a hill and to a sign post. Up the hill were the upper falls, and down the hill were the middle and lower falls. I chose to go up first, and began the small hike. If not for my hungover status, I would have enjoyed the slightly strenuous walk.

As I wound my way up, the falls suddenly came into view, the sound of falling water deafening. I scooted along the dirt and rocks to get a closer look, and found myself looking down from near the top of the falls. There were a few people scattered along the rocks below, taking pictures of themselves and their groups, but for the moment I was alone. Watching my step, knowing how dangerous loose gravel could be, I sank down on a boulder and enjoyed the view. Above the falls, a walking bridge stretched from cliff to cliff. After this first drop, there was a space of flat rapids before another drop further down.

Deciding to explore more, I continued up the hill, reaching the bridge. There were steps to the left, leading up to what looked like the highest point I could get to. Steeling myself for sore muscles, I climbed the stairs, waiting to look around until I'd reached the top.

I wasn't disappointed. From here, I could see some of the falls, the trees in the valley below, and the lake once again. It was simply gorgeous up here, and I knew without a doubt that I would be back.

Going back down the steps, I continued up the path, leading away from the falls, curious what else I would find. I walked along a winding dirt trail, stepping over tree roots and skirting around boulders, loosely following the river, calm on its journey to the falls. When I stopped, I walked carefully across rocks to perch on another boulder. Slipping off my shoes and socks, I stuck my aching feet happily into the water. It was cold, even for being so shallow, and a welcome relief. There wasn't another person in sight, and as I sat, slowly moving my toes up and down in the refreshing water, I felt a calm come over me that I rarely experienced. Days like this, I could understand why people chose to willingly live in a place as cold as this one.

When I walked into work that night, I was tired, yet upbeat. I'd managed to grab a short nap after coming home from my excursion, and the peaceful feeling that had filled me had yet to leave. It even made me feel assured enough to face Dominic.

I was pretty sure.

Gabi was in the locker area when I entered, and we did our normal girlish squeal in greeting.

"You look good!" Gabi seemed more surprised than she should. "Did you get some sleep?"

"No," I grinned. "I went hiking."

She gave me an incredulous look, which I took to mean she was questioning my sanity. I shrugged, not caring.

"Dominic's here," she leaned close to whisper. "I saw him, and he was all polite to me, like we didn't *just* see each other last night."

"That's weird," I told her. In truth, the fact that he spoke to her at all was what was weird. "Where are you tonight?"

"Cosmetics," she rolled her eyes. "I asked for PMDF."

"Maybe next time," I attempted to bolster her, but went to check the schedule for myself. Clocking in, I waited to walk with Gabi out into the main store.

"Tim texted me," she was excited by this.

"That's great," I told her, and I almost meant it. "Have you talked to Jake?"

"Yes," she rolled her eyes. "I finally gave in, and told him I'd moved on and he should too."

"How did he take that?" I asked.

"Well, he called in tonight, so we'll see what kind of messages I get later."

With half a smile, I waved as Gabi veered off towards her section, and made my way back to the coolers.

Only Kade and I were scheduled for PMDF, though he had been grabbed to help with the main truck unload, so I was on my own for a while. Starting with the freezer to get it out of the way, I geared up and trudged inside.

Over the weeks I'd been doing this, my body had become slightly acclimated. It was definitely easier now than it had been the first night, though I still shivered uncontrollably for several minutes when I was out. Tonight was no different. When I emerged from the silver door, I stood for a moment, breathing deep and thinking warm thoughts. Walking towards the prep room, I removed the oversized suit before slipping my jacket back on. When the door opened behind me, I spun with a grin on my face to greet Kade.

"Thank goodness you're here," I began, but snapped my mouth shut when I saw who it actually was.

"Now, that's the kind of greeting I prefer."

Dominic watched me, assessing either my mood or my attire, I couldn't be sure.

"What do you want?" I asked with narrowed eyes.

"I came to help you," he grinned infuriatingly. "Kade will be a while."

"Fine," I turned, pulling my gloves back on. "I'm going in the produce."

"That's fine," he said easily. "I'll go in the meat cooler. We can handle dairy together."

For some reason, I swallowed hard at the thought.

Without another word, I grabbed a cart and pushed it inside. I worked slowly, which was unlike me, and felt petty. With a sigh, I lifted a box of strawberries into the cart, knowing it was the last of the batch. I'd stalled as much as I could.

Trudging down the hall to the dairy cooler, I took a deep breath and opened the door.

He was already inside, and didn't bother to look up when I entered. Not letting that bother me, I logged into the batch and went to my first location.

Since two of us were logged in, it started me at the back of the batch- which was the juice and milk areas. Without protest, I began lifting the heavy items from the shelves. I was on a ladder, balancing precariously with the scanner in one hand and grabbing milk jugs with the other, when his voice spoke from beside me.

"Why don't we switch?"

A strangled gasp escaped my throat, losing my balance for just an instant, which had my arms flailing back. For one terrifying moment, I envisioned myself falling, slamming into the shelves behind me, all the milk coming crashing down on top of me.

Strong arms wrapped around my waist, easing me gently to the floor. The scanner went hurtling to the floor, as did the milk I had been grabbing. One lightning quick hand snuck out, palming the milk as if it weighed nothing more than a feather.

There was still an arm wrapped around my waist, which I enjoyed more than I was willing to admit, and I turned to stare at my rescuer with wide eyes.

"Thank you," I breathed.

We were so close I could inhale his scent. I did so gladly.

"You're welcome," he was watching me carefully, not making any attempt to move.

Suddenly, I realized I was standing in a cooler at work, in the very personal space of my boss.

Jumping back, I scrambled for something to say, something to do to distract from the moment we'd just had.

"Um," I glanced down, seeing the scanner still in one piece. Though I stooped to grab it, he beat me to it.

"Here," he held out his instead. "I was going to ask if you'd like to switch, so I can work on the heavy stuff. And now, after your near-death incident, it's only right."

Not being able to speak, I nodded. "Of course, if you hadn't scared me, I wouldn't have fallen," I finally reminded him.

He smiled his partial smile, just the edge of his mouth tipping up. It made my knees weak.

Accepting the scanner from his hand, I made my way to the front of the cooler.

"How are you feeling?" He asked, apropos of nothing.

Startled, I turned to stare at him again. "What?"

"After last night. How are you feeling?"

A blush crept up my cheeks, spreading down my neck. With a glare, I spoke my mind.

"Yeah, what *about* last night?" I asked. "What, exactly, were you doing there?"

He looked surprised by the question. "I was out having a drink."

"At the very bar I *happened* to be at?"

"Yes," he answered me slowly, not seeming to understand my line of questioning. "Purely a coincidence."

With a frustrated grunt, I turned back to my work. "That doesn't explain why you decided to get all macho."

When he spoke, his voice was beside me. How did he move that silently? I did my best not to flinch.

"I was concerned for you. You are one of my employees, and you were not in your right mind. What would you have me do?"

Refusing to meet his eyes, I merely shook my head. He was twisting my words, giving me perfectly logical explanations for events I'd overthought. I wasn't buying any of it.

"I'm a big girl, I can take care of myself," I spit out instead of arguing.

"Reese," he said my name gently, waiting for me to meet his gaze. When I did, I wished I hadn't. There was something swirling in the green depths, some emotion I couldn't put a name to. "I know you can take care of yourself. However, I'm old fashioned. It's how I was raised. So, when I see a damsel in distress, I can do nothing but see to her needs."

There was so much unspoken in his comments, and I searched his expression to give me a clue as to what it was I was missing. "I don't understand you," I finally answered him.

His lips curved infinitesimally. "I know."

With that, he moved in his silent way back to the other side of the cooler to finish the batch.

95

CHAPTER 10

The next night of a food tuck, I was in the prep room with Kade and Jesse, explaining my ideas to help us run more smoothly.

"Half the stuff we pull doesn't fit out on the floor, which means its sitting out for no reason, and it's doubling our work since we just have to put it back again. So, I was thinking, at least for produce and meat, we go to the floor first and write down everything we need, grab it, knowing we're getting the oldest stuff first. Then, after the truck comes and we get everything stacked in place, we go through and wipe everything from the locations and re-enter it in the system."

"That would actually be faster," Kade seemed on board.

"Give it a go," Jesse shrugged. "I'll handle the freezer."

"That's why you're our favorite," I told him with a wink.

Grabbing a pad of paper from the drawer beneath the sink, I headed out to the floor while Kade tackled the dairy cooler. I was positive my idea would work, and save us time and headaches.

Jotting down everything I needed, I went to the back to load up, crossing off the items we had on hand. When the truck came in, we could backstock it and just grab the things we needed, instead of bringing full pallets to the floor.

I was pretty sure I was a genius.

My other idea I had taken from softlines, when they sorted everything into carts. When the frozen and dairy was unloaded, we could sort it the same way. Yogurt with yogurt, cheese with cheese. That way, everything would be backstocked together, too.

Dominic wasn't around tonight, and for that I was both disappointed and grateful. Sandra was in charge, and I'd seen Jacob around, though he didn't speak to me much now that Gabi and I were friends and she'd broken it off with him.

After I was done with the produce and dairy, I helped Jesse with putting out the frozen, then we both helped Kade finish in dairy. The truck showed up just as we were finishing, between our two breaks.

Explaining my ideas to Kade, Jesse and Sandra, they all seemed willing to give it a try. After the four of us had everything sorted and stored in the coolers, it was time for lunch.

"I'll have two more people come help put the truck away," Sandra told us. "Will that be enough?"

"The way we've split it up, I think it will," Kade answered her.

We were all feeling unusually optimistic about a task that had always been dreaded.

Gabi also had the night off, so I sat with Jordan. Unlike with Gabi, where the conversation rotated around people, and her boys in particular, Jordan and I talked books, travel and TV shows.

Before sitting, I stopped by the table the cleaning crew was lounging at, eating leftovers of food that had me missing the southwest.

"¿Cómo estás?" I asked.

Rosa gripped my hand, patting it as she answered. "¿Muy bien, y tú?"

"Bien, bien," I squeezed her hand with a smile. "Enjoy your lunch."

Sliding into my seat by Jordan, I hadn't even pulled out my phone and she was talking.

"Oh my gosh," Jordan was unusually upbeat. "I just started an amazing book, you have to read it if you haven't already."

"Sure, what is it?" I asked, loving new recommendations.

"The author's name is Valerie Reed," Jordan told me, and I was stunned.

Valerie Reed was a pen name, the name I used to remain inconspicuous. Jordan was reading my books, and recommending them to me? I couldn't stop the wide smile from blooming.

"I've read some," I confided, playing it down but not wanting to pretend ignorance.

"Isn't she amazing? I've never been one for romance, but when I'm reading hers I don't feel the need to gag."

Laughing, I appreciated the sentiment.

"Would you believe my mom got me to read it? Normally, we don't agree on *anything*."

"That is impressive," I told her.

After that, we lapsed back into silence, and I couldn't help the small glow her praise had inspired.

Heading straight back to the coolers after lunch, I set to work with my list while Kade concentrated on dairy with his helper, and Jesse on frozen with his helper. Since I'd filled in most of the produce already, I only had one small cart to bring out to the floor. The same thing happened with the fresh meat, and I spent a good chunk of time organizing both coolers, wiping them clean in the system before re-entering the information. I'd written numbers on the outside of the boxes, showing how much of each item was inside, and the entire process easily cut my time in half.

Once I was done, I found Kade in the dairy cooler. There was only one cart remaining to go to the floor, so I stayed and began backstocking the extras. It wasn't long before Kade came in to help, sending the extra help away. Once we were done, Jesse, Kade and I finished up the freezer. We barely all fit with the extra carts, but we made it work.

All said and done, we'd cut the time it took to put everything away by at least a third, if not more. When the three of us walked out of the back room, Sandra looked impressed.

"That was fast," she commented. "I think we've definitely found a new way to do the food truck."

"Nice going, Reese," Jesse clapped me on the back.

It made me inexplicably happy.

In a race, I sprinted across the flat land of Iowa, my body a smooth machine made for the freedom running granted. My competitor was on my tail- literally- and I pushed myself harder.

Though he was older, by about three minutes, I was faster.

The terrain became rocky and hilly, signaling our arrival at our favorite place to play. Other boys played football, or videogames in their parent's basements; for my brother and I, this was true happiness.

Just as we were reaching the waterfall, a devastated scream ripped through our minds, faltering our steps. We both tumbled to the ground, skidding to a stop. With one long look between wolves, we turned as one and raced back the way we came. This was no longer a game. Lives depended on our speed.

We were too late. Our parents were gone.

From this day forward, we were no longer children playing. We were men, with a vendetta.

The next night, Gabi was back at work and had a new guy texting her all night. This one's name was Ian, and they'd met at yet another bar.

"What happened to Tim?" I asked, catching myself in time to call him by his name, and not Jerky.

"We had one fun night," she waved her hand as inconsequential. "Ian graduated from college last year, and is such a sweetheart."

Shaking my head, I ate my salad and took a good look around the room. Dominic was there, but not in the breakroom. I still didn't know where he went during this time, and I tried hard not to ponder it too long.

"Oh, guess what! My friend Pearl will be in town this weekend, so I told her we'd meet up for dinner."

Glancing back at Gabi, I asked, "Who's Pearl?"

"Oh, we grew up together in Sun Valley. I've known her since we were in diapers."

Gabi had told me about her hometown, somewhere south of here, in Wisconsin. I couldn't imagine growing up in a town that didn't even boast a drive-thru.

"That sounds fun," I told her. "What's she in town for?"

"She's coming for a visit with her sister to meet up with their cousin, I guess she's driving through. I haven't seen Pearl in *forever*."

"What day?" I asked, worried I'd be working.

"Next Friday night," Gabi told me. "I already checked, you have the night off."

"All right," I told her with a laugh. "I guess I'm in, then."

"What are you doing *this* Thursday?" Gabi asked next.

"Something with you?"

"Yes! See, I was talking to Ian, and he has this friend…"

I groaned. "Ugh, Gabi, please, no."

"Come on," Gabi begged. "Just this once. I want you to meet Ian, anyway, and I don't want you to be all alone."

"Is there anything I can say to talk you out of this?" I asked hopefully.

"Nope!"

Letting out a sigh, I agreed. "Fine."

"Yay!" Gabi shrieked. "Meet us at Coral Reef, around 8:00."

"Can't wait," I mumbled. My lack of enthusiasm went straight over her head.

It was Tuesday, and I had the next two nights off. Since I'd be spending Thursday with Gabi and the setup, I decided to spend Wednesday cleaning and doing some shopping. The rough draft for the novel was going well, and I'd already sent several chapters to my editor. She was happy with them, too, and I knew I was on the right track.

CHAPTER 11

The bar I was meeting Gabi and her new boyfriend at was on the waterfront, just off the downtown area. Stepping out of my car, I was easily distracted by the bright glow of the moon over Lake Superior. There was something about the expansive collection of water that pulled me in, and I briefly considered spending my night standing at the railing, watching the waves crash upon the shore.

Steeling myself for the setup that was about to ensue, I turned away from the enticing view and pulled open the door to the bar. The main room was large, several tables set up by the windows next to a small open dance floor and a karaoke machine. Since this was a weeknight, the machine was, thankfully, silent. A square bar sat in the center of the room, and beyond that, a smaller room held a couple of pool tables, dart boards and another space for dancing.

"Reese!" Gabi grabbed me in a bear hug, spotting me immediately.

She had jumped up from one of the high round tables along the windows. Her boyfriend, along with his friend I was going to 'love,' sat at the table.

"Come on, meet Ian and your date!" With a firm grip on my hand, Gabi dragged me to the table only a few feet away.

Gabi draped herself across a blonde man with a slight build. "This is Ian," she announced with a flourish.

"Hey, Ian," I greeted her boyfriend with a handshake before turning to his friend.

Since he was sitting, I couldn't be sure on his height, but he seemed to be shorter than myself. He had dark, curling hair and tiny eyes behind a pair of glasses. Normally, I didn't judge someone based on appearance, but his lack of eye contact and the fact he didn't stand to greet me already rubbed me the wrong way.

"Hi, I'm Reese," I extended my hand.

"Gavin."

Taking my hand briefly in his, I felt as if I were shaking a wet noodle.

"Sit here!" Gabi gestured to the open chair between Gavin and herself.

"What'll you have?" Ian asked me, and I perused the bar quickly.

"Rum and coke," I told him. After my chocolate martini night, I'd renewed my ban on alcohol, and wanted something I could pretend to sip on without anyone noticing the liquid wasn't going down. Later, I could ask the bartender to refill it only with soda.

Ian headed to the bar and Gabi followed him, so I tossed a smile Gavin's way. He was watching his drink studiously, and I tried some easy conversation.

"Are you from around here?" I asked.

He nodded, without so much as a glance in my direction.

"Gabi told me you were in the military," I tried again. "Where were you stationed?"

"Thailand," he answered.

This piqued my interest. Travel was always something I could connect with another person on.

"That's awesome. I've heard it's beautiful there."

He nodded again. Holding back a sigh, I accepted the drink as Ian returned.

"Thanks," I told him.

"No problem," he responded before turning his attention to Gabi.

Taking a small sip, I worked at getting more than a one-word answer from my date. "What did you like about Thailand?"

He shrugged. The hand in my lap squeezed into a fist, nails biting into my palm.

When I looked to Gabi for help, I realized they were making out. As my brain began running through excuses to leave early, my eyes swept the inside of the tavern. There was a dark figure leaning against the bar, watching me with an amused expression plastered on his face. Zeroing in on the chiseled features, I felt a red blush creeping up my neck.

Of course he was here. Desperate now for a way out, I nudged Gabi.

She broke from her kiss, shifting her eyes dreamily to me. "Gavin, Reese told me she's always wanted to go to Thailand. You should tell her about it."

As she spoke, butterflies began slamming against the soft lining of my stomach. Without raising my head, I knew *he* was approaching the table.

"Dominic!" Gabi gushed. "What are you doing here?"

"Good evening Gabi, Reese. Gentlemen," he greeted our entire group, though his gaze remained steady on my face. The unwelcome blush was still very much in evidence. "I was having a drink at the bar, and thought I'd come say hello."

Ian shook his hand, and after introductions, Dominic turned to Gavin. "And you are?"

"Gavin," he answered, offering the same limp shake as he had with me.

Dominic shot me a look with a raised brow, and I shrugged, puzzled by Gavin's lack of social skills.

To my surprise, Dominic glided around the table to stand directly between my date and me. His wild scent immediately enveloped me, and I found myself taking a deep breath in, wanting to hold it in my lungs. He was so close to me I could feel heat radiating off his skin. On a cool night like this, I wanted to snuggle into his warmth.

Snapping out of my wayward thoughts, I snuck a glance at Dominic, but he didn't seem to notice my shortness of breath or heart that suddenly decided to go haywire.

"I apologize, did I interrupt your conversation?" Dominic asked smoothly.

"Gavin was just talking about his time in Thailand while he was in the military."

Gavin bobbed his head up and down. "There were garbage cans lining the streets."

It was dead silent for several beats.

"Garbage cans?" I finally broke the silence.

"Like, in rows," he expanded, apparently finished with his story.

With wide eyes, I looked around the table. Gabi and Ian were embraced once again, so my gaze could only land on one other. Dominic and I shared a look of utter bewilderment.

"That's... interesting," Dominic finally spoke up. Clearing his throat, he changed the subject. "I see you have cat hair on your jacket. Do you have a cat?"

"I do!" Gavin looked up, excitement on his face. "I have three cats. They're so funny to watch."

My jaw dropped open. I'd been attempting a conversation with this man for the last 15 minutes, and cats were the way in?

"Hey man, cats are cool. What else do you like to do?"

"Play video games," Gavin told Dominic.

As they got into a discussion on the better gaming system, I sat listening, completely taken aback. Somehow, I had become the third wheel on my own date.

Gavin excused himself after several minutes to use the bathroom, and Dominic immediately turned to me, leaning an arm against the tabletop. His gravity was sucking me in again.

"Interesting company you keep," he smirked as my eyes narrowed.

"Gabi set me up," I mumbled, glaring at my friend, who was oblivious to us.

Dominic held his hands up, palms facing me. "I'm not judging."

"Yes, you were," I shot back, then sighed. "He literally said two words to me before you came over here, but you two seem to be hitting it off. Want me to leave so you can have some privacy?"

This wiped the smirk from his face momentarily. "You're not enjoying yourself." It was a statement, not a question.

"What was your first clue?" I muttered.

"You also haven't touched your drink," he observed. Picking up the glass, he took a sniff. "Rum and coke?"

Shrugging, I played it off. "I'm not much of a drinker. Usually," I amended, embarrassed at the memory it dredged up. "Plus, I have to drive home."

"Right," Dominic studied me. "To your sister's."

This took me aback. I'd mentioned my living situation once, when I first began working. How had he remembered that?

"That's right," I answered hesitantly.

Gavin returned then, and I stood. "It was nice to meet you, Gavin, but I really need to go."

Gabi took a breath from her lip lock to grab my arm. "No! You can't go yet!"

"Sorry, Gabi, family emergency." As I patted her hand in reassurance, I avoided Dominic's amused expression. "You guys have fun."

Pulling on my jacket, I began to make my way around the table and to the freedom of the outside.

"Gavin, aren't you going to walk Reese out?" Dominic asked, forcing me to pause and gawk at him.

"She parked right in front," Gavin stated, seeming flabbergasted by the question.

Dominic stared at him for a beat before joining me, placing one hand on the small of my back and gesturing towards the door with the other. "Shall we?"

Gulping, feeling the searing heat of his hand right through my clothes, I allowed him to lead me out the door.

"You didn't need to walk me out," I finally managed once we were in the cool night air. It felt good against my suddenly warm skin.

"Pretend, for a moment, that I'm a gentleman," Dominic's lips quirked up into a half smile.

We approached my car, and I looked longingly towards the water. The moon had risen substantially since I'd been inside, and it left the whole area aglow.

Dominic noticed my gaze and spoke again. "Would you like to stay and talk for just a little while? It's a beautiful night, after all."

My eyes met his, and I was hit with another round of butterfly wings as two dark emeralds glittered down at me. Without rational thought, I found myself nodding in agreement to his suggestion.

His body relaxed at my acquiescence, and I realized he'd been holding his breath. Why would that be? It was almost as if he were... nervous.

Without another word, we walked towards the path directly behind the bar, that was part of the larger walkway that led around the lake. I leaned against the railing, keeping my body forward. Dominic mimicked the pose next to me, and I was surprised at the comfortableness of the silence between us.

"Tell me more about yourself," Dominic spoke first.

The question startled me, and I glanced up at him. "What would you like to know?"

"Anything," he answered immediately. "You don't share much about yourself. That can be frustrating."

I grinned at him, bordering on a laugh. *"I* don't share much? Mr. Tall, Dark, and Mysterious says *I'm* frustrating?"

"Even now, you're evading," he turned towards me, raising a brow. "Tall, dark and mysterious, you say?"

Laughing fully now, I slapped his arm. "Don't let it go to your head."

"Wouldn't dream of it," he studied me, waiting for me to speak.

Sighing, I raised a shoulder before letting it drop. "I've moved around a lot. It hasn't left room for me to have close friends. Over time, I've become my own council, so yes, it's difficult for me to open up."

"You've got secrets," he mused, rubbing a hand across the stubble along his jaw.

"Doesn't everyone?" I asked pointedly.

"Touché," he responded easily. "Can I make an observation?"

For some reason, I began to feel uncomfortable and worried about what I was about to agree to. "All right."

"Your resume said you'd worked in retail before, but you were completely clueless when you started. Not that you didn't pick things up right away," he clarified, "and even come up with more streamlined systems for a couple of the areas, but it was obvious this work was new to you. That begs the question, why would you lie?"

My mouth popped open to respond, but he wasn't done.

"You're clearly very intelligent, and you study the people around you. You move like someone weighing 20 pounds lighter, you have two car seats in your car but the seats themselves and floor are immaculate. Even though you live with children under 5 years, I can't pick up the scent of baby powder and you look well rested for someone who spends half their sleeping time supposedly awake and babysitting."

His spiel done, I found my mouth was still hanging open, but no reply came.

"How is any of this any of your business?" I finally spit out, my eyes blazing with fire. "And, if you want to talk about inconsistencies, let's talk about you for a minute. You ask questions of people at work like you're interrogating them, yet refuse to answer any about yourself. When we're at work, you ignore me as often as possible, yet decide to play the hero tonight. You move like a jungle cat," I paused, realizing I was in dangerous territory. My voice softened, the fire quickly dispersing. "You observe people and situations like it's your job. If you think *I've* got secrets, maybe you should look in a mirror."

The night had become perfectly still as we stared at each other. Though the fire was gone, sparks still flew. This man was so frustrating. He showed up every day looking sexy as all get out, ignored me half the time and ticked me off the other half, then had the audacity to stand here and tell me that *I* was hiding something.

It didn't matter that he was absolutely right, about everything. My secrets were my own, and he had no right to call me out on them.

Suddenly, his mouth tipped up, and to my amazement, he let out a low, deep laugh. It was the first time I'd heard him truly laugh, and it did crazy things to the ever-active butterflies in my stomach.

"It seems we're at an impasse," he observed. "Perhaps, one day, you'll trust me enough to tell me the truth."

"Ditto," I shot back.

Hesitating just a moment longer, I spun on my heel and stalked to my car. Slamming the door, I glanced back once to where I had just been standing, but he was gone.

CHAPTER 12

Another week went by, and while I was feeling incredibly comfortable at work, the silent battle with Dominic left me constantly on edge.

There were so many times I'd caught a glimpse of a good, decent person inside his hard exterior, but in a blink, it was gone, replaced by the aloof and annoying man he was.

Even after we'd had it out at the bar, nothing between us had changed. If anything, he became even more closed off. He was the most frustrating person I'd ever met.

Finally, after several days, I'd managed to put the strange event behind me. I came into work and was asked to help in the back room for the first part of the night. I agreed, though I'd never done that before, but Sandra assured me it was exactly like in the coolers. Grabbing a scanner, I made my way back, keeping an eye out for someone I knew well enough to ask. Luckily, I found Jesse, who bounced between the back room and PMDF.

He showed me the ropes, loading up a batch for me and pointing me to the correct aisle.

The tiny aisles were a little scary, with towering shelves on either side, close enough to touch both simultaneously. Steep ladders, attached to the shelves, looked treacherous.

It wasn't long before I had to test one out.

Using my logic skills, I reminded myself that if these things could hold a bear of a man like Jesse, it wouldn't have trouble with me.

Taking a deep breath, I climbed up, scanned what I needed, and carefully lifted the box to my shoulder. Making it back to level ground, I let out the breath I'd been holding.

Checking my next location, I sighed when I realized I'd be going back up.

Placing one foot in front of the other, I climbed once again to the top, staring at the large box my scanner told me was needed. Setting the scanner down on a shelf, I maneuvered the box with both hands, edging it closer to me each time. It wasn't as heavy as it was large, and I knew I could handle it, as long as I could get a good grip.

I took one look around, seeing if there was anyone around I could ask for help, but the walkway was empty.

Back to jimmying the box off the shelf, I focused, determination set on my face. Unbeknownst to me, the large box I was manhandling was hooked to another box, and just as I realized that, they both came crashing down. My natural reaction was to jump out of the way, except I was on a ladder, and there was nowhere to go.

One second, I was facing my doom, boxes mere inches from my head, body flailing. The next, I was in the far corner, wrapped in steel, boxes smashing to the ground.

I stared in disbelief, my mind unable to comprehend what had just happened. My pulse pounded in horror of what had almost transpired, and finally, I glanced down.

The steel that had me in a vice grip were arms, and my feet were barely touching the floor.

"Wha... What..." I began mumbling almost incoherently.

In a swift move I was released, but my knees buckled and I found myself restrained once again.

"Breathe. Breathe, Reese, it's okay. You're okay."

The words, the voice were urgent, but I was still unable to piece together recent events.

We moved then, and I found myself leaning against the shelves, facing my rescuer. My impossible, sexy, frustratingly indifferent rescuer.

"What just happened?" I breathed, staring into Dominic's strained face.

"I caught you as you fell," he answered, expressing something with his eyes that his words belied.

I shook my head, whether in denial or trying to clear it, I wasn't sure.

He bent his head to my level, staring intently into my eyes. "Are you all right? You seem like you're in shock."

"You... you weren't near me. How... how did you get here so fast?"

My voice was barely above a whisper, and I wondered if he was right in that I was going into shock. Glancing back to where the boxes lay haphazardly on the floor, I gasped in realization that I should have been under them.

Dominic straightened suddenly, pulling me off the shelf to stand on my own. "Tell them you're fine," he whispered harshly.

Confused again, I looked up at him to ask what he meant, but was stopped by Jesse and a couple of others standing at the end of the aisle.

"Reese! What happened? Are you all right?"

"Fine," I called out. "I'm fine," I repeated, my voice stronger. "It was a close call, though."

"I was walking by when the boxes began to fall," Dominic added. "She's fine, but she won't be doing work back here anymore."

My eyes shot to his, incredulous.

"Go," he said it quietly, just for me. "I'll take over for you. Help on the floor." Then, louder, he addressed the small audience we'd gathered. "Back to work, guys. Everything's fine."

Once everyone had dispersed, Dominic gave me a gentle nudge, and I stumbled out of the aisle, feeling numb.

I made my way to the bathroom, first, and splashed cold water on my face. When I looked in the mirror, my eyes were wide and my face was pale. What had just happened?

In a daze, I walked back to the main group, going blindly into an aisle. It was only when I was halfway through the boxes piled on the floor that I realized I'd chosen the candy aisle.

My shock was wearing off, and the questions that swirled were making me almost angry.

As I was getting close to being done, Dominic stepped into my view. He stood close, picking up one of the boxes left.

"You're fast. Like, inhumanly fast," I hissed at him, ripping open a box of Jelly Belly's.

"Keep your voice down," he admonished me, scooping up bags of gummies to slide onto pegs.

"My voice *is* down," I shot back in a harsh whisper. "And you're avoiding."

"I just wanted to make sure you were all right. I shouldn't have left you alone like that when you could have been in shock."

"I'm fine," I told him quietly, the rage slowly escaping. "But, I want answers."

He sighed, leaning his head briefly against the metal shelf. "This is not the place."

Pausing for a moment to take in my surroundings, a laugh bubbled up, catching us both by surprise. Sobering immediately, I shot him a sharp look. "Name the right place, then. We're going to have a real talk."

Closing his eyes, he took a deep breath and I realized he was as riled up as I was.

"After work," he finally responded, spinning on a heal to exit the aisle, leaving a half empty box of skittles in his wake.

Glancing down at the bag of M&M's in my hand, I took a moment to come to grips with reality. No one in my life had had the ability to fire me up like that insufferable man.

The rest of the night seemed to drag on. Gabi wasn't there, and I found myself missing her incessant bubbly chatter. If anything, it would have helped to take my mind off the evening's events. Instead, I was left with nothing but my own thoughts. Dangerous territory, indeed.

When lunch finally arrived, I settled into my usual seat, greeting Noah, Becca and Jesse before opening the container with salad that was supposed to be my meal. My appetite had disappeared, and I stared dejectedly at the lettuce until I felt the familiar tingle along my skin signaling *he* was in the room. Fighting my natural reaction to glance up, I quickly lost, sneaking a look from under my lashes. His eyes were on me, and I immediately focused back on the table.

In a move that was very unlike me, I lay my head on my arms and closed my eyes, blocking out not only Dominic, but everyone else.

The rest of the night went by in a blur, my moves robotic. As I was finishing the last of my work, tension began kicking in. I was about to have a real, honest conversation with Dominic. Excitement and nerves at the prospect began a tango, wreaking havoc on my stomach lining.

Walking slowly towards the time clock, I methodically typed in my number for the last time this shift. One look around told me Dominic was nowhere to be seen. Do I wait for him? Hang out in the parking lot?

A whole new level of stress worked its way into my already strained system. Maybe I could just leave. He owed me an explanation, and I'd get one, but it didn't necessarily have to be now.

I'd completely talked myself out of staying when I opened my locker, and found a slip of paper, folded in half, resting inside. Unfolding it carefully, I read through the neat scrawl incredulously.

Something came up. I promised you a talk, and I will hold to my word, it just can't be today. Stay safe.

I was, at turns, annoyed, relieved, and, finally, thrilled by his final words. *Stay safe.* In his own maddening, irrational way, he cared.

Placing the folded paper into my purse, I grabbed all my things and headed out the door. The sun was attempting to peak through a thick layer of dark and roiling clouds, propagating a summer storm. As I thought it, a rumble of thunder reverberated through the ground, resounding in my chest. Pausing beside my car, I stared at the sky for a few moments. Thunderstorms had always fascinated me, though I preferred to watch them through a window, snuggled under a blanket with a good book in my lap.

With a smile, I got in my car and hurried home. That was exactly how I would spend my morning.

I ran inside just as the thick drops began to fall. They splattered against my head, cool against my skin. With a grin towards the heavens, I bolted inside and snuggled into my chair, book in my lap. This window afforded views of my backyard forest, and the constant streaks of lightning backed up by the boom of thunder gave it an ethereal feel.

For a long time, I stared out the window, not even glancing at the book I held in my hands. As another flash of lightning illuminated the stand of trees, I let out a gasp, shooting out of my chair to press my nose to the window.

123

There, at the edge of the trees, stood the magnificent gray wolf from my dreams. Though it stood in the center of a storm, it was stoic, its body still while its eyes looked straight at me.

That was silly, I admonished myself.

And yet...

For several long moments, we stared at each other through the pane of glass. I was enchanted by its majesty, the dreams I'd been having flitting through my mind's eye.

In another instant, another streak of lightning, he was gone.

With a shuddering breath, I sank back into my chair, eyes wide. For a long time I waited for the creature to return, but the storm had ended, rain pattering down consistently in its stead. Finally shaking myself out of the moment, I took a quick shower to remove the dirt of the night and went straight to bed. As always, my thoughts flashed to Dominic as I succumbed to sleep.

CHAPTER 13

When Gabi and I walked in to the bar-restaurant together, she immediately spotted Pearl. The two obvious sisters waiting for us, with their blonde hair and sparkling green eyes, had me feeling instantly self-conscious. They were sitting at a high table, with several empty seats available. Pearl jumped up and ran to the entrance, nearly barreling Gabi down with a hug.

"Oh my gosh, it's been so long! You look amazing," Pearl gushed, and while they continued to shriek at each other, I glanced over with an amused expression at Pearl's sister, Jade.

Gabi had given me the rundown on the two, along with some amusing stories from their childhood, on the drive here. Pearl was a stay at home mom, and Jade was a photographer. When I asked what their last name was, Gabi had told me the person I was meeting was none other than J. Callaghan.

I'd been a fan of her photography for a long time, and found myself a little nervous to meet her. That wasn't the main reason for my sudden self-consciousness upon seeing these two sisters, however. They were both *gorgeous*.

To my surprise, Jade was staring at me with a shocked expression on her face. With a surreptitious glance down at myself to make sure I'd not forgotten anything important, like shoes or pants, I couldn't find anything amiss to warrant such a look from a complete stranger. Any amount of self-consciousness that I was feeling promptly doubled.

Before I could turn tail and run, Pearl grabbed me in a hug. "You must be Reese, I'm so happy to meet you! Come meet my sister, Jade, she's right over here," she continued to talk at top speed, and I found myself being pulled along by the hand. I had a feeling most people found it difficult to say no to this woman.

I was almost afraid to look at Jade again, but when Pearl introduced us, her face had composed itself into a welcoming smile. Shaking hands, I still wondered what her initial reaction had been about.

Pearl and Gabi sat beside each other, and I quickly became lost in their hometown gossip. Feeling sorry for me, Jade scooted around the table to sit beside me.

"They'll go on like this for hours, trust me," Jade confided, sending her sister an adoring grin. There was obviously a lot of love between them, and I felt a ping of envy that I did my best to squish. "Are you from here?"

"No," I answered Jade. "I've lived a few different places, but came here to help out my sister."

Her eyes narrowed just slightly, as if she could tell I was lying. Swallowing hard, I decided to turn the tables. "I know your work," I confided. "I've been following you for years."

"Thank you," a genuine smile stretched across her face.

"You're from Sun Valley?"

"That's right," she told me. "Though, I left for several years as soon as I was able. I recently went back, and decided to stay."

"Does that ring have anything to do with that decision?" I gestured towards the monstrosity gracing her delicate hand.

Her bright smile was contagious. "A little. My fiancé, Talon, will be joining us in a little while."

"Fiancé?" Gabi's head spun, eyes zooming in on Jade's left hand. "When did that happen? Anyone I know?"

"Talon moved to town after you left," Pearl filled her in. "And he's really hot."

"Oh, tell me more!" Gabi didn't bother to let Jade finish, and turned back to Pearl for the juicy details.

"She tells it better anyway," Jade laughed. "But to answer your question, even though I loved living other places, I'd forgotten what it was like to be around family. I missed it."

"You guys have a big family?"

"You have no idea," Jade rolled her eyes. "Last week was our annual family picnic, and this year we had over 200 people."

"Two hundred?" I choked. "Just in your family?"

"Mom came from seven and Dad came from twelve," Jade grinned at my surprised look. "There's four in our family, Pearl and I have two older sisters, plus, Pearl's popped out seven just on her own."

Jaw hanging open, I glanced again at the woman in question. *Seven* children? And she still looked happy, not stressed out?

"We're actually here meeting a cousin of ours, she just got a fancy job in California. She's driving from Boston to California, so we decided to meet up with her for one of her stops."

"That's really cool," I told her, intrigued by the dynamics of such a large, and obviously close, family.

"What about you? Just the one sister?"

"Yeah," my eyes drifted down, a strange sadness overcoming me. "Just the one."

"Are your parent's around here, too?"

"No," I told her. "They passed away when we were young."

"I'm so sorry," Jade touched my arm in sympathy, and crazily, I felt my sudden melancholy begin to lift. My eyes met hers, and I could have sworn a smoky mist swirled in the green depths for just a moment. But then I blinked, and it was gone.

Pulling my arm away, clasping my hands together in my lap, I watched her carefully. There was something strange about this strikingly beautiful, empathetic woman.

"So, how long have you been engaged?" I asked in an attempt to shift the focus of conversation.

Another smile lit Jade's face. "About nine months. If it was up to me, we would have just eloped in Vegas, but that's not how things work in my family."

"I imagine not," I commented.

"What about you? Boyfriend, fiancé?" She winced when she said this, and instead of answering, I gave her a quizzical look. "Sorry," she explained, "I used to hate when people asked me that. Plus, if you're single, Pearl will have you set up with someone before we leave this bar."

Her admission made me laugh. "Well, I am single, but let's not tell your sister that. Gabi's bad enough as it is."

"We heard that," Pearl swung towards me. "And, it just so happens, I know the perfect man. He's on the chubby side, but most of that is big muscles, and… "

"No need," Gabi piped in. "Reese already has a man."

Her assumption made me turn red, and my denial came out more forceful than I intended. "No! I mean, no, I don't."

"Oh, that definitely means there is one! Jade used to evade us about Talon just like that. Spill!" Pearl honed in on me like a bloodhound.

"Uh, well, there's nothing to tell," I stammered, unused to such attention.

"His name is Dominic, he's one of the managers at work," Gabi happily threw in.

"Is he good looking?" Pearl turned to her friend.

"Super-hot," Gabi confided. "But, kind of scary. Really serious type, always glaring at people with his arms crossed."

"Which just kind of makes him hotter?" Pearl asked.

"Right!" Gabi exclaimed.

Somehow, though the conversation was about me, I had suddenly become a third party.

"Ignore them," Jade told me. "I always have."

"There's not really anything going on between us," I tried to explain. "He actually drives me crazy, not in the good way. We scream at each other more often than not."

With a knowing smile, Jade placed a hand on my arm. Then, too quickly for me to know if I'd made it up, she leaned towards me and sniffed. She immediately sat back, eyes wide and apologetic.

"I'm so sorry," she began, "I can't believe I just did that..."

Trailing off, her attention was diverted. Her head turned towards the wall as if someone had called her name, and though I glanced to where she was looking, I saw nothing but empty booths.

"I'll be right back," she told me hurriedly, rushing out of the restaurant.

Pearl and Gabi didn't even seem to notice her abrupt absence, and it only took me a moment to decide to follow her. Standing, I excused myself and walked quickly to the door. Glancing around the parking lot, I didn't see her anywhere. This was getting stranger and stranger.

Rounding the corner of the building, there was a large expanse of grass leading up to the inevitable woods. The sun was setting, lending the tall trees even longer shadows. Jade stood near the woods, speaking heatedly with a dark skinned, extremely attractive man.

As I took a step forward, they both turned to me. With a sheepish smile, Jade glanced at the man before speaking to me.

"Reese, sorry for leaving so quickly. This is my fiancé, Talon."

If this was her fiancé, why did they seem to be arguing?

Talon approached me, extending a hand. "A pleasure. My apologies for arriving late, I had some business to take care of."

When our hands touched, I couldn't help but notice how warm his skin was. Eerily similar to Dominic's, though I'd only made direct contact once, I'd only been close enough several other times to feel it coming off him in waves, or burn right through my clothes.

Crossing my arms after a brief shake, I looked between the two. Talon had moved protectively to Jade's side, placing a hand on the small of her back. Though they weren't showy about it, there was so much love between them. It was subtle, yet easy to see in each lingering touch, their bodies constantly shifting towards one another. Each glance between them seemed like it held an entire conversation.

Though I'd known many happy couples, none seemed to click as effortlessly as these two, which made the conversation I'd interrupted even more perplexing.

"Is everything okay out here?"

They looked at each other once before Jade answered. "Yes, everything is fine. Why don't we go inside?"

"I'll join you in just a minute, I left something in the car," Talon began to excuse himself, but then a giant shadow descended on all of us.

My neck craned up, wondering what could make a shape like that, but there was nothing above us. Confusion clouding my face, I looked back at Jade and Talon, but they were now back to back, eyes sweeping the woods beyond where we stood.

Fear slid along my spine, more for the fact that nothing since I'd walked into this dinner had made any sense. Wondering if I was still in bed, having some kind of lucid, vivid dream, my eyes began searching our surroundings.

"What... what is going on?" I asked in a trembling voice.

Talon whipped his body to face me, but his focus was past me. I turned, barely registering his low aside to Jade.

"Take her inside, keep her safe."

Jade's hand clamped on my wrist, but I was facing the same direction as Talon, watching a shape fly through the trees. It took too long for me to register what it was I was seeing, and before my eyes could take the image and shove it into my brain, Jade's grip loosened, and I found myself several feet away from the couple. A form stood before me in a crouch, both arms out as if protecting me. A low growl startled me out of my momentarily frozen posture.

"Get away from her," the deep voice snarled.

In an instant, Talon was in a similar position in front of Jade, his face transforming from underwear model to terrifying.

In a quiet, tentative voice, I spoke.

"Dominic?"

CHAPTER 14

"Dominic?" My voice came out so quietly, I wasn't sure he'd be able to hear me.

Though absolutely nothing in my current predicament made sense, I knew instinctively that I had to diffuse the situation. Reaching out with one hand, I wrapped my fingers around his forearm.

"Dominic, it's me, Reese." Feeling a bit ridiculous, I plowed on. "These are my friends, Dominic. Please don't hurt them."

"They're dangerous," he spat, not relaxing his position.

Talon watched me curiously, though his body was tense, ready for a fight. From behind him, Jade observed both of us with interest.

"Dominic, look at me," I coaxed the man who seemed more animal than man. "Please, just look at me."

His head turned just slightly, and though he frightened me in that moment, I straightened my shoulders and spoke softly.

"These are not bad people. Just relax, and if you want me to leave with you right now, I will."

Talon straightened, trusting me to handle the dangerous creature that stood in our midst, though he still held Jade back with an arm.

Dominic zoomed in on the movement, eyes narrowing. "The only time I've come across my kind, it has not ended well."

His kind? What in the world was he talking about?

Talon opened his mouth to respond, but snapped it shut as another shadow passed over us. Dominic and Talon shared a look, any animosity suddenly gone as they both straightened and faced the woods.

Jade approached me, grasping my arm once again. Completely baffled, I attempted once more to reach Dominic.

His head whipped towards me, making eye contact for the first time. "Go inside. I need you safe."

His words struck a chord in me, warming my insides in a way that was both pleasant and infuriating.

"Come on, Reese," Jade coaxed me, but I was having none of it.

"Not until someone tells me what the hell is going on!" I finally burst out.

Go inside now!

It was Dominic's voice, but it wasn't spoken out loud. His voice was *inside* my head, and as I watched, Dominic and Talon took off into the woods.

Jade was pulling me away, so instead of stumbling around, I turned to follow her. When I glanced back once more, they were gone.

When we were back inside, I stood in the doorway and felt my limbs beginning to shake. Jade placed her hands on either side of my face, giving me something to focus on besides the bizarre events I'd just witnessed.

"What's going on? What was that? Where did they go?" I knew I was babbling, but could do nothing to avoid that.

"Reese, I need you to take deep breaths so you don't hyperventilate," Jade's voice was low and urgent. "Take a deep breath in, let it out slowly."

Following her directions, I sucked in a breath and blew it out.

"That's good, let's do a few more," Jade encouraged.

After a few more deep breaths, I closed my eyes briefly while Jade released her grasp. Opening them again, I started my questioning in a calmer manner.

"Please explain to me what is going on."

Jade glanced around, making sure we were alone for the moment. Spotting someone walking towards us, Jade dragged me to a spot well away from Pearl and Gabi, and anyone else in the bar.

"How well do you know Dominic?"

"We... we work together," I told her.

"Are you two dating?" Jade asked.

"I wouldn't call it that," I answered her. "There's an attraction between us, but nothing more."

"Did he... did he speak into your mind just now?" Jade seemed hesitant to ask this.

And here, I was hoping I'd made that up. "I... I think so. But that's *crazy*. People can't do that."

Jade's eyes tightened just slightly, as if she was the last person wanting to deliver this news.

"Some people can," she finally said.

I tried to process this, and my mind instantly spun out. All the things I'd noticed about Dominic that just seemed off, now came back at full throttle.

"He's something different, isn't he?" Excitement warred with fear and confusion. "Are," I trailed off, not quite able to believe I was about to spew this in front of a complete stranger. "Are vampire's real?"

Jade's mouth turned up at the corner. "Not exactly."

"What does that even mean?"

"Reese, you deserve an explanation, but I'm not sure I should be the one to give it to you. Talon and Dominic are on their way back."

Eyes wide, I asked the obvious, "How could you know that?"

She tapped her head discreetly. "Some people can communicate differently."

The door opened, and the two men walked in. Talon went directly to Jade, and as they examined each other for signs of injury, my eyes met Dominic's.

His expression was a hard mask, with just the slightest trepidation showing through. As I continued to gaze into his stormy gray eyes, I felt myself sinking into their depths, the world around us simply disappearing.

"We should go somewhere we can talk in private," Jade snapped me out of the intense gaze.

No one said a word, so I finally spoke up. "We can use my house. No one is around."

"Let me talk to Pearl," Jade said, turning towards her sister and Gabi.

"I should say goodbye to Gabi," I commented to no one in particular.

"Let Jade handle it," Talon stopped me from leaving. "Will you be all right driving?"

"I'll drive her," Dominic's deep voice suddenly spoke up. When I opened my mouth to protest, he silenced me with one look.

"Let's go," Jade smiled upon returning. "We'll follow you."

Surrendering my keys once we were in the parking lot, I slid into my passenger seat, but remained facing Dominic. For a while I watched his profile silently, brimming with questions yet unable to formulate any of them into words.

"I know you have some questions," he began.

"That's an understatement."

137

"Are there any I could answer right now?"

"What was that shadow?" I asked the first thing that popped into my mind.

His eyes cut to the side, assessing my expression without turning his head. "That might be the more difficult thing to explain."

"All right, how were you able to talk to me... inside my mind?"

I watched his eyes tighten. At least he wasn't going to deny that had happened.

"Reese, I'm not like you," he began, and my brow furrowed, but I let him go on. "You've noticed other things, and I know I owe you an explanation about last night, but I need you to listen to everything I say and not freak out."

"Why would I freak out?" I asked sardonically. "Just because absolutely nothing tonight has made any sense?"

This time, he turned to fully look at me, and realized I was attempting to lighten the situation with a bit of humor. The tenseness in his arms relaxed just slightly.

"I have special abilities," he spoke quietly. "I'm able to control the elements. Fire, water, air and earth. I'm also incapable of reproducing blood, and have to intake it regularly."

Digesting this information, I responded lightly, "Like a vampire?"

The corner of his mouth tipped up. "If that helps you process this, then yes, like a vampire. Except I'm not undead."

In a surprise move, he gripped my right hand, pulling it across both our bodies to rest my palm against his chest.

"Feel that?" His voice whispered across my skin as I felt the pulsing of his heart through the thin material of his shirt. "My heart beats, my skin is hot." Overly so. My earlier comparison of his skin to Talon's was accurate. He released my hand from his grip. "My people are called Elementals. There are not many of us left, and more that are turning into the shadow creatures that you witnessed tonight."

Now we were getting somewhere, though he skipped my second question and answered my first.

"Those shadows were people?"

"In a way, yes. The shadowmen, as we call them, are Elementals who have given into the darkness. Given up their souls."

Taking another moment to think through this, I glanced out the window and realized we were pulling into my driveway. With narrowed eyes, I glared at Dominic.

"How did you know where I live?"

With the first smile I'd seen all night, Dominic let out a low chuckle that did crazy things to my insides. "I've always known."

Shoving that bit of information to the back of my mind for the moment, I stepped out of the car and walked to my front door, with Dominic, Talon and Jade on my heels. Walking into the main room, I gestured towards the dining table. "Make yourselves comfortable."

"Why don't I make you some tea?" Jade offered. "It'll help calm your nerves."

"That sounds great," I told her, touched by her thoughtfulness. "Kitchen's through here."

Leading her through an archway into the back of the house, I showed Jade where the teapot and tea was and left her to it. When I stepped back into the front of the house, there was some kind of silent showdown going on between the two men. Standing between them, though closer to Dominic, I attempted to diffuse the situation once again.

"Dominic and I talked briefly on the way here," I said to break the silence. Facing Talon, I continued, "He told me what Elementals are. Does that mean you're an Elemental, too?"

"I am, as is Jade." With a sigh, Talon relaxed his posture and softened his tone. "Dominic, I apologize for believing you were a shadowman. Your appearance just after the shadow led me to that conclusion."

"I'm still not convinced," Dominic was still glaring.

I looked at him with shock. "You fought together, didn't you? Plus, look how in love with Jade he is. You can't possibly believe he gave up his soul."

With a defeated sigh, Dominic ran a hand through his hair. "Apology accepted. And," he eyes cut to me once, "I also apologize for attacking you."

The two shook hands, and I let out a sigh of relief. "Can we please sit now, like civilized people?"

"Tea's ready!" Jade sang out, carrying a tray with cups and the teapot.

"That was quick," I rose a brow at her.

Talon laughed, wrapping an arm around Jade's waist once the tray was safely on the table, pulling her onto his lap. "Did you use your abilities to make the water boil faster?"

"Yes," Jade was unrepentant. "It's a neat trick," she grinned at me.

Though I was processing all of the information that had been thrown at me over the last hour, I was still fascinated.

Settling into her own chair, Jade poured cups for everyone.

"First of all, we haven't been properly introduced. I'm Jade Callaghan, this is my fiancé, Talon Wolfchild. My family is from Sun Valley, but Talon grew up in the southwest."

"My name is Reese Valentine," I told them, then looked to Dominic. He remained silent, so with a roll of my eyes at his dramatics, I spoke for him. "This is Dominic Drake." Then, glancing at the bronze skinned man, I asked, "Where in the southwest are you from?"

"Mainly in what is now New Mexico," Talon answered, "but I imagine that raises more questions than it answers, so we can come back to that."

"Okay," I turned towards Dominic, needing something familiar in this odd conversation. "We talked a little in the car about what Elementals are, but where do they come from? Are you turned into one?"

"I was born one," Dominic answered me. "Though, certain people can be changed."

Talon spoke next. "My mother was Elemental, but my father was not. I was born into a half-life, and eventually changed. My mother chose to die when my father's natural life was done, so I spent many years without any of my kind."

I was lost again, but I knew there was a lot of ground to cover here and I would be patient.

"Talon changed me, more out of necessity than anything, though I would have worn him down eventually," Jade explained.

"So, anyone can become Elemental?" I wanted to clarify.

"No," Dominic answered for them. "Only one of the Gifted."

Closing my eyes, I took a sip of the cooling tea before asking the obvious. "What, or who, are the Gifted?"

"Individuals with latent abilities. As an Elemental, I can sense those who are Gifted, feel a connection to them, and other Elementals. We have been more on guard recently with these shadowmen," Talon answered me. "Until I met Jade, and another female Elemental friend of ours, I didn't even know they existed."

"Of course," Dominic groaned. "They're after the women."

"All women?" I gasped.

"No," Jade told me gently. "Elemental and Gifted women."

"So, I don't have to worry..." trailing off, I registered the looks on everyone's faces. Focusing on Dominic, I asked him the question with my eyes what I was afraid to voice aloud.

"Yes," his voice was gruff. "You are one of the Gifted."

Standing abruptly, the chair knocked to the ground behind me. Without a word, I tore through the house, into the kitchen and out the back door, leaving three perfect strangers alone in my dining room.

CHAPTER 15

There was no thought behind my escape, I'd simply hit my limit on the supernatural. It was one thing to hear about it, it was quite another to realize I was part of that world.

Running for the tree line, somewhere in the back of my mind I realized darting into the woods, after what I'd witnessed tonight, was not the brightest idea I'd ever had, but I continued on. Feet pounding down the familiar path, I ran until my breath came out in gasps and I was forced to halt. Holding myself up with a palm against the trunk of an oak tree, I tried to breathe deep and fight back tears that were threatening to spill.

A leaf crunched beside me, and I closed my eyes, knowing who the intruder was. My treacherous heart began to race, pulse pounding so hard I could feel it in my wrists.

"Go away," I whispered pathetically.

"I can't do that," the gruff voice replied.

He didn't touch me, and for that I was grateful. One touch from him, and I would crumble.

Resting my head against the tree, I struggled to get myself under control. Swiping under my eyes for any stray tears, I turned to face Dominic.

"I'm sorry," I mumbled. "I think I've hit my weird limit."

"That's understandable," Dominic soothed. "This is a lot to take in."

"And there's more," I said, and it wasn't a question. I knew we hadn't even scratched the surface.

"There is," Dominic answered me. "But it can wait."

There was an undefinable expression on his face, a mixture of fear, curiosity and longing. I didn't know what my face looked like in this moment, but I felt my emotions mirroring his.

"Just tell me," I finally sighed. "Get it all out in the open right now so I can process."

He was silent so long I wasn't sure he'd respond. Then, more gently than I thought him capable, his palm rested against my cheek. The heat from his hand seared into me, and at once I felt my whole body relax.

"I was able to speak into your mind because we are connected," he finally spoke.

"Connected how?"

He dropped his hand from my face, sliding down my arm to clasp my hand. "I'd rather you came to your own conclusion. I'd rather you came to me because you want to, of your own free will, not because you felt you had to."

"Dominic?" His name was like candy on my lips. "Do *you* want *me*?"

"I have since the day we met." His honesty was my undoing.

Stepping up to him, feeling a sudden influx of strength in his admission, I pressed my lips to his. Electricity hummed around us, and as he took control, one hand against my lower back while the other wrapped itself in my hair, I could have sworn actual sparks began to fly. He lifted me until I had no choice but to wrap my legs around his waist. Before I knew we'd moved, we were inside my house, his body pressing mine into the soft mattress.

A single thought broke through, and I lifted my head with a gasp. "Jade and Talon..."

"Have left," Dominic brushed fingertips across my cheek, his eyes dropping down to my slightly swollen lips. "We are alone."

"Good," was my only response, running my fingers through his hair before pulling his lips back to mine.

Lying in my bed with Dominic's strong arm wrapped around my waist was pure bliss. This was the most at peace I'd ever felt, and I didn't want anything to change.

Because of that, I stayed quiet, staring at the ceiling with a small smile playing at my lips.

"What are you thinking about?" The soft whisper of breath tickled my ear.

"How perfect this moment is," I turned to face him, snuggling into his chest. "Why did we wait so long to do that?"

"I think, because you hated me."

Rolling my eyes, I slapped his shoulder lightly. "I didn't hate you. You just annoyed me."

"Not sure that's better," he narrowed his eyes at me.

"Admit it, I annoyed you, too."

"You did," he acknowledged. "You have no idea how many times I wanted to shut you up with a kiss, or," he slapped my butt playfully, "beat you into submission."

With a teasing gasp, I scooted away from him. "You wouldn't dare."

"Try me," he grinned easily. This was the most carefree I'd ever seen him.

Though I didn't want to move, my stomach had other ideas. It grumbled, loudly, which made me wince.

"Hungry?" Dominic asked with a raised brow.

"Starved," I told him. "We never actually ate dinner."

"Leave it to me," he said, rolling off the side of the bed.

"You cook?" I asked, a little too surprised.

He managed to look charming and sheepish. "Ah, no," he pulled on a pair of jeans. "But I do know how to order pizza."

"Sounds perfect," I told him, standing also. "I'm just going to wash up."

Escaping into the bathroom, I shut the door and turned to stare at myself in the mirror. There was a glow to my face that was a testament to Dominic's attentions. There were faint smidges of bruises at random parts of my body, and as I brushed my fingertips lightly across them, how they came to be replayed in my mind.

Finding myself flushing with the memory, I quickly turned on the shower and, after it heated, stepped under the hot spray. I needed a few minutes to myself to think, and a shower was as good an excuse as any.

The logical part of my brain had flown out the window as soon as I'd attacked Dominic in the woods. Though I wasn't proud of that, I didn't regret it, either. But, now that my senses had returned, I had a lot to sort through.

There were people with extraordinary abilities to manipulate the elements. They drank blood to survive. Something about what Talon had told me, about how he grew up in 'what was now called New Mexico,' made me believe they also lived longer than normal. I wasn't ready to confirm that aspect, but would ask the question eventually.

The bigger bombshell, was that *I* might have special abilities. That *I* could become an Elemental.

Dominic was also holding something back from me, something big and important. He'd told me he wanted me to come to my own conclusion, and that he wanted me to choose him of my own free will. I'd definitely done the latter, but as for the former, only time would tell.

There was one thing I knew, and it gave me the confidence to walk out of the bathroom to face Dominic again. He wanted me, just as much as I wanted him. For now, that was all I needed.

149

CHAPTER 16

Wrapping myself in a towel, I stepped out of the bathroom and found Dominic still lying in my bed. With a tentative smile, I lay beside him, my skin pink from the heat of the shower.

"Hm," he murmured, brushing his fingertips along the line of the towel. "You should always wear this."

Letting out a laugh, I rolled my eyes. "It's a towel, not clothes."

"Yeah," he placed his lips at the intersection between my neck and shoulder. "Only this."

As I felt myself beginning to melt, there was a knock on the front door.

"Don't move," he breathed, and was gone before I could blink. That would take some getting used to.

I heard him exchange a few words with the delivery person before he returned with a box of pizza in his hand.

Narrowing my eyes, I asked, "When did you put on a shirt?"

"Before I answered the door. Wouldn't want anyone to start rumors, now, would we?"

"But… you were laying here... without a shirt."

He stilled, watching me carefully.

"What? What is it?"

Shaking his head, he moved at a normal pace back to the bed. "Nothing. Just waiting for you to freak out again."

"Oh," I blinked at him, waiting until he was sitting cross-legged before I spoke. "I don't think that'll happen. And, really, finding out the stuff about you, and Talon and Jade, was kind of cool. It was just when it became about me that I started to hyperventilate."

"I have a feeling you'll always surprise me," Dominic shook his head, popping open the top of the box.

As the aroma of tomatoes and spice wafted out, I inhaled appreciatively. "That smells delicious."

Standing, I pulled on a t-shirt and shorts before joining him back on the bed. Lifting a piece out of the box, I took a bite while I contemplated my next set of questions.

"I've never done this before," I commented first.

"Done what?"

"Sat on a bed and ate pizza," I told him. "It's kind of fun."

"You know what would make it better?" He asked.

"What's that?"

"Bad 90's sitcoms," he answered.

I laughed, then held up a finger. "I have just the thing!"

Scrambling out to the living room, I pulled out a box of items that had been left by the previous tenant. Inside was the fourth season of Fresh Prince of BelAir, on DVD.

Bringing it back into the bedroom, I popped in the first DVD and settled back onto the bed.

"That is the most random thing," Dominic commented. "You just had this laying around?"

"It was here when I moved in," I laughed. "Just the fourth season."

"Cheers to that," he held up a 2-liter of soda, that had been delivered with the pizza, in a toast before passing it to me. "Want some pop?"

"It's soda," I told him matter-of-factly.

"Try again. You're in Minnesota, and you have no argument because of that."

"Doesn't matter!" I exclaimed. "It's a short name for soda-pop. If you have a friend named Jonathon, you call him Jon, not 'athon.'"

"What about Isabella? You would call her 'Bella,' not 'Isa.'"

"'Isy' is also perfectly acceptable," I pointed out.

"Agree to disagree," he gestured with the bottle still in his hand. "That didn't answer the question, though."

"Yes, I would like some," I grinned, accepting the bottle and taking a swig.

Once he set the bottle down, I turned serious. "You know I have more questions."

"I know," Dominic took another slice of pizza. "There's no secrets between us now, Reese. You can ask me anything."

"You have a long lifespan?"

"Yes," Dominic answered. "Though, I didn't lie about my age. I'm twenty-five, and am only now coming into my full power. It takes us longer to mature."

"What happened to your parents?" This was a difficult question, but I needed to know.

He sighed, pausing the video. "They were murdered. By a shadowman. My brother and I have been hunting him since that night, four years ago."

Wrapping my arms around him, I held him close. "Oh, Dominic, I'm so sorry," I murmured.

He let me embrace him for a few moments before gently taking my hands, holding them between us. "They were good people. They tried to raise my brother and I as normally as possible, and that was their downfall. Instead of using their powers to protect themselves, they tried to be human."

"Tell me about your brother," I said quietly.

154

"His name is Emerson. We're twins, as are most offspring of Elementals. We've been inseparable until recently. We got two different leads at the same time, which brought me here, while he took off to Europe. I hated splitting up from him, since we're stronger together, but it seemed necessary."

His thoughts had turned inward, and I let him be for a few moments.

"Tell me more about him," I finally prompted.

"We're a lot alike, though he's more serious, if you can believe that. Twins have a special connection."

He seemed to hesitate, so I encouraged him. "What kind of connection?"

"For one, we can communicate telepathically."

"So, you can talk to him in your mind. Like... like you did with me."

He nodded, watching me cautiously.

"Do you have to be close to do that? Or could you talk to him now if you wanted?"

"Distance has not been a problem," he answered. "We can also combine our powers when we're close to each other."

It took me a moment to process that. "Combine your powers? What powers? Like element manipulation?"

"It's more than that, but yes. All Elementals have several things in common, element manipulation being one of the things."

"Along with needing blood to survive and living a long life?"

"That's right," he approved. "And most, though not all, will have talents that go above and beyond."

"What's yours?" I asked.

"I can tell when someone is lying," he told me with a smirk. "You, in particular, lie a lot."

Blushing, I looked down at my lap. "Not anymore," I promised.

"My brother's talent is a little bit darker. He can cause pain, through the mind."

With an inward gasp, my eyes widened. "That's terrible."

"In the wrong hands, yes. But he's the most moral person I know, almost to a fault. If anyone should have that power, it's him."

"All right," I paused, thinking through that.

"You can manipulate electricity," he said suddenly.

"What?!" My voice was louder than intended. Lowering it a few decibels, I tried again, "What are you talking about?"

"Did you honestly not feel that, in the woods? Sparks were, literally, flying."

My jaw worked, but no words came out.

"And once we came inside, the lights dimmed several times. That lightbulb," he pointed towards the hallway, "Burnt out."

"I guess I was distracted," I blushed again. Damn him and his ability to embarrass me.

With a gentle hand, he lifted my chin to look into my eyes. "It's nothing to be ashamed of. Your ability, or the fact that we made love."

We searched each other's eyes for several long moments, until I eventually leaned forward to press my lips to his. Pizza forgotten, I shifted forward, pressing against Dominic's hard chest. His arms wrapped my waist, shifting me onto his lap.

Before I could get too lost, I pulled back to meet his gaze once more. "I still have questions."

"I'm sure you do," he grinned.

"You said you had a lead that brought you here."

He nodded. "I believe a shadowman is using Wilson's as a cover for running drugs."

This surprised me. "That's what you do on breaks," I muttered to myself.

"Yes, and why I seem to be questioning people at work, as you so aptly put it. Now, though, I think it's your turn to answer some questions."

Biting my lower lip, I knew I couldn't get out of it. "Oh, I figured this would come up eventually."

"I've been completely honest with you. It's your turn."

Sighing, I leaned back, though I remained on his lap, quietly reveling in the ability to do so. "My name is Reese Valentine. But, I'm also known as Valerie Reed."

"The writer? You're a writer?"

There was an incredible pleasure in the fact that he'd heard of me. "Yes. For my next novel, I strayed away from things I've done to tackle a new subject. Vampires."

He was silent for several beats of time. Then, he let out a loud laugh, his body rocking with amusement to the point that I had to wrap my arms around his neck to stay secure.

"You came to Duluth, of all places, to research *vampires*?"

"Yes," I wasn't appreciating his laughter as much as normal. "It's dark for long hours during the winter, cold- because why would the undead care about that? Plus, I feel like vampires would like all the wilderness around here, but there's still easy access to people. You know, for food."

"Those are some very good points," his eyes still glittered with amusement.

Crossing my arms, I rose a brow. 'You're forgetting the most important thing. I found *you*. And Jade, and Talon. So, obviously, I was right."

He sobered immediately. "You have me there."

Self-satisfaction coming off me in waves, I asked, "What else would you like to know?"

"This whole back story of yours, the sister, the moving around, none of it is true?"

"I'm an only child," I confirmed. "After my parents passed away, my grandmother raised me, but she passed away when I was 19. She refused to talk about them, and I never had anyone else to ask."

"I'm so sorry, Reese," Dominic placed his palm against my cheek. It made me feel cherished. "And the moving around?"

"That part is true. This might sound extreme, but I like moving to a new place, experiencing the people and the culture, and use it to write my novels."

"That's why they seem so real," Dominic murmured, as if to himself. His eyes met mine sheepishly. "I'm not much of a reader, but your books spoke to me. Now I know why. I've read them all."

That fact sent a thrill through me. "You have?"

He nodded. "A secret pleasure of mine. Not even my brother knows, he would probably make fun of me."

"I modeled the vampire in this story after you. Before I knew, you know..." I waved my hand at him, encompassing his entire being.

"Really?" His grin quickly turned playful. "And, this vampire, does he fall for the girl?"

"Oh, yes," I smiled back.

His hands slid up my rib cage, his thumbs brushing against my most sensitive areas. I let out a gasp, arching into his touch.

"Let's see if I can inspire you some more," Dominic whispered, bringing my face back to his.

CHAPTER 17

"What's this?" I asked, picking a paper up off the dining room table.

Dominic padded silently into the room, wearing only his jeans. My eyes drifted to his bare chest, instantly sidetracked.

"Jade left her number for you," he told me. "She said they would be in town a few days."

"That was really sweet of her," I commented, putting the paper down again. Though it was well past the middle of the night, we were both wide awake. I blamed the overnight shift; Dominic had other reasons.

"When do you sleep?" I asked him.

"Rarely," he replied. "We get lethargic for a few hours in the afternoon, but if we need to be awake we can be. Sleep heals us, though," he explained further.

"I wonder why that is. Why you're tired in the afternoon, I mean."

"Not sure," he leaned a hip against the table, facing me. "I've never thought about the science behind it before, it's just how it's always been."

"When you say sleep heals you…"

"Our bodies can withstand more than the average human. Physical injuries which should take days to heal, will only take hours. Sleep, and an influx of blood, both speed up the process further."

"That is seriously cool," I commented offhand. "What else can you tell me?"

"Making notes for your book?"

I flushed, my eyes dropping to the ground. "Maybe. Though, I'll have to rethink this one a bit. Now that I know I'm writing more non-fiction than fiction..."

Trailing off, I glanced back at Dominic's face. He was smirking at me.

"What?"

"You're too cute," was all he said.

It sent a strange, unfamiliar buzz through my chest.

"Well, I have to take these things into consideration. I don't want anyone taking my novel too seriously. That could be dangerous for you. And for me," I tacked on.

He nodded gravely. "That is true. Stick to the traditional undead, burning in the sun and all that. You'll be better off."

At this point, I couldn't tell anymore if he was being serious or mocking me. Deciding to give him the benefit of the doubt, I changed the subject.

"What now?"

"What do you mean?"

"In general, I suppose. Now that we've," I gestured towards the bedroom, "done that, are we considered dating? Should we keep it hidden from people, at work? What about the shadowman you tracked down earlier tonight? Are there more of them? Do I need to be worried?"

He held his hand up, palms towards me. "Slow down," he advised. "First, yes, if you agree, we can consider us 'together.' I'd rather not tell anyone at work just yet, since I am technically your manager. This job is a means to an end for both of us, but I'd rather not jeopardize it in the meantime. Lastly, there was one shadowman earlier tonight. Talon has him secure."

Dominic's brow furrowed at this, and I decided to skip directly to why. "You don't agree?"

"These are bad men," Dominic told me flatly. "I've never taken one hostage."

With a gulp, I set my gaze on the opposite wall. This man, who had such a gentle and tender side, was also terrifying.

"Why did Talon?"

"He believes Jade can fix him."

This caught my attention. Whipping my head back towards him, I asked, "How could Jade fix him?"

"Apparently, she's done it before. She's an empath," he elaborated. "I've never met one before, though, to be fair, I don't know many of my kind as it is."

My thoughts flicked back to the bar, when Jade had put her palm on me and I'd felt my sorrow being sucked away. If what Dominic was saying was true, I hadn't just imagined that.

"What does an empath do?"

"We didn't have much time to discuss it further," Dominic told me. "But, I'm sure you'll be able to ask her."

Glancing at the number, I picked up the paper again. "Why don't we ask now? They'll both be awake, right?"

Dominic took a pointed look around the house, and our lack of clothes. "Perhaps we should clean up first."

After straightening the house, and replacing the lightbulb that had mysteriously burnt out, I pulled on the same outfit from when I'd gone to dinner and made the call.

"Hello?" Jade answered on the second ring.

"Jade, it's Reese. I hope I'm not bothering you."

"Of course not! I'm so glad you called. Are you all right?"

"Yes, I am," I assured her. "I was wondering if you'd like to come back over? We might have some more things to discuss."

"We'll be right there," Jade promised before hanging up.

Wrapping my arms around Dominic's back, I pressed into him, merely for the fact that I could. He didn't ask any questions, just pulled me closer, his cheek resting atop my head.

164

We stood like that for only a few minutes when there was a knock on the door.

"Boy, she wasn't kidding," I commented, opening the door to Jade and Talon. "You guys are quick."

One look outside had me realizing there was no extra car. Jade noticed.

"It's faster without the car," she explained.

Gesturing for them to enter, I noticed Jade's small smile when she looked between Dominic and I. Slightly embarrassed, I went to sit beside him.

Don't be embarrassed, Dominic's voice popped into my head. *It's a natural part of life.*

Wide eyes shot to his. "How do you *do* that?"

Jade laughed at my outburst. "I see you haven't discussed *everything.*"

"No," I told her. "But enough. I'm sorry for running out earlier. It was a lot to take."

"Believe me, I understand," Jade said. "I was in your shoes a year ago."

"And you accustomed beautifully," Talon put in. "As will you, Reese."

"Dominic told me about the shadowman, that you think you can help him. How?"

Clasping her hands on the table, Jade began to explain. "I'm what's called an empath. I can connect to people using their emotions. Not only am I able to read them, I can," she glanced at Talon, seeming unsure of how to explain, "go into another's mind."

There was silence for a beat. I broke it.

"I'm sure that's not easy to explain, but can you try?"

Jade nodded. "The first shadowman we came across was named Frances. I was new into this life, and didn't know what I was doing, but I reached out to him with my mind and could see his memories. There was darkness everywhere, but I kept searching through it, looking for any speck of light. When I finally found it, it led me to a room where a small boy was huddled. When I led the boy out of the room, the darkness cleared for him."

"She's skipping the part where she became trapped in the room," Talon's demeanor darkened.

"But, you found me," Jade smiled, leaning into him to kiss his cheek.

"That's incredible," I breathed.

"It truly is," Dominic answered. "Where is this Frances now?"

Jade and Talon shared a look, smiling at some inside joke.

"He's with a friend of ours named Lani. Though he's been on this earth longer than me, what Jade did seemed to revert him to his childhood. It's like he's been given a second chance at life, a child in a man's body."

"This is difficult to believe," Dominic commented.

"It's amazing," Jade spoke up. "And, kind of fun for us to watch. Our friend Lani, well, she's not used to being around people at all, so watching her deal with a man who acts like a teenager, it's been entertaining."

I smiled with them, but Dominic was having a harder time seeing the levity.

"A shadowman killed my parents," he said quietly. "Each one I've come across since has been evil."

"Dominic, I'm so sorry," Jade's hand moved towards Dominic, but he backed away from her contact.

"I know you mean well, but my emotions are what fuel me. I'd rather not lose them."

Placing my own hand on Dominic's arm, I slid down until our hands clasped. It was a gesture meant for solidarity, and also a reminder that these two were on our side.

Since Dominic fell silent, I decided to change the subject. "How long will you be in town for?"

"After we meet with Jade's cousin, we had planned to continue on to the southwest. Lani and Frances are out there now," Talon answered.

"We could stay here for a little longer, though," Jade commented. "If you'd like us to."

Glancing at the silent man beside me, I tried something I'd been curious about. He's spoken into my mind, it was only logical that I would be able to speak back.

Focusing on his features, following the same trail that he'd used, I pushed my thoughts into his head.

Should we tell them about your suspicions at work?

At first, I wasn't sure that it had worked and I felt ridiculous, as he gave no indication that he'd heard me. Then, his voice fluttered against my mind, sending heat waving through my limbs.

Well done. For now, no, I'd rather keep that between us.

"How soon do you plan on visiting the shadowman? To see if you can help him?"

Jade answered that one. "This morning. It takes a lot out of me, so I should be able to rest before my cousin is due to arrive."

"How are you able to allow her to be in harm's way?" Dominic directed this at Talon.

Jade jumped on that before Talon could respond. "*Allow* me? I'm a strong, independent woman and I don't need anyone *allowing* me to do anything!"

Talon placed a placating hand on her arm while I smirked, enjoying someone else yelling at Dominic for a change.

"Just be glad she doesn't have an iced tea," Talon commented, sending a loving look to his fiancé. "To answer your question, it is difficult for me to see her put herself in dangerous situations, but, as you can see, she will do as she wishes. I have found a way to help her, joining together to become stronger."

"I apologize, I meant no offense. I was raised a bit old-fashioned."

"It's fine," Jade waved it off. "Talon gets pretty overprotective, too."

"What you were saying about joining together, is that like what you can do with your twin?" I asked, directing the last towards Dominic.

"It sounds similar," Dominic nodded.

"I'm unfamiliar with the connection between siblings, as I am an only child, but from the stories my mother told me, I believe so. Twins and mates both have a strong connection."

There were several pieces of information floating around in my mind, attempting to assemble into one coherent fact, but before I could latch on to one thought, it was gone again.

"I'd like to be there when you meet with the shadowman," Dominic announced, diverting my attention once again.

"*We'd* like to be there," I corrected.

He shot me a glare, but I ignored him.

I can't let you be in harm's way.

Too late, I'm in this whether you want me to be or not.

169

He let out a frustrated groan, crossing his arms with a scowl. Jade sent me a meaningful grin.

"Why don't we go now?" Jade asked. "No time like the present."

CHAPTER 18

Dominic and I drove to the location Talon had given us directions to. Since I let Dominic drive, I was free to gaze out the window, still processing everything I'd learned tonight. He remained silent as well, though I could only imagine what was running through his mind.

Jade and Talon had their own way of getting there, which they assured me was quicker than by car. Talon also insisted Jade eat first, to bolster her strength. Actually, he's used the word *feed*, but for my sanity, I was preferring to believe he meant *eat regular food*.

"Will you be all right?" I asked as we began to slow down. "Seeing the shadowman?"

"Yes. I will also be able to discern whether he is lying or not, which should be beneficial."

I nodded, staring out the window again. In less than 12 hours, my whole life had been flipped upside down. Supernatural creatures existed, and I was now sleeping with the man beside me, who also happened to be one of those creatures. He could speak into my mind, which was one of the most intimate things I could imagine, and I was able to speak into his. We were about to question, then try to save, a shadowman, who was the epitome of darkness.

Yet, with all of that to sort through, I couldn't stop remembering the feel of Dominic's rough hands against my soft skin, his lips pressing into mine...

"Whatever you're thinking about, could you wait until after we interrogate the shadowman?" Dominic's velvety voice interrupted my daydream.

171

"What do you mean?" I asked, startled.

I can smell your arousal, his voice purred into my mind, his words making me blush furiously. *It is very distracting, and I need to concentrate.*

Sucking in a deep breath, I directed my thoughts away from where they wanted to go.

"Is that it?" I asked, spying a small building ahead. We were on a dirt road, well north of my house. I was already on the outskirts of town, so it didn't take long to completely leave civilization behind.

"Yes," Dominic answered. "I can hear them."

This brought me up short. If he could hear them, they could hear us. "What is this place?"

"An abandoned building. Talon has ensured no one will come near."

Though I was burning with curiosity, I didn't ask how he had managed that.

We stepped out of the car, and I was suddenly on edge. This was all way out of my realm, and I began having second thoughts of being here. Then, Dominic wrapped his hand around mine, and I instantly felt grounded. Smiling up at him, I had the courage to walk inside.

Talon and Jade were already inside, standing over a man who sat in the corner, head in his hands. Jade glanced over at us, motioning us to stay back.

"What's your name?" Jade asked softly.

There was no response.

Talon crouched, draping his elbows over his knees and clasping his hands together. "We can help you, if you allow us. Tell us your name."

The man raised his head, spitting daggers of hatred at first Talon, then Jade. When his eyes landed on me, I let out a gasp and stepped backwards. There was pure evil in his eyes, evil that I hadn't truly known had existed. Dominic squeezed my hand, stepping in front of me to block me from the shadowman's view.

"You can't help me," he spit out, his focus back on Talon.

Feeling like a wimp, I stayed behind Dominic, wrapping a fist in the back of his shirt.

Jade looked at Talon, and as some unspoken communication passed between them, she closed her eyes and took a deep breath. Dominic was on full alert, watching the scene with interest and disbelief. Talon had risen to stand beside Jade, one hand resting on the small of her back. Though they were both standing before me, I could tell they weren't really in the room with us anymore.

Several minutes passed in absolute silence. Suddenly, the shadowman let out an anguished cry, gripping his head again. A part of me wanted to reach out to help, but I remained rooted, secured to Dominic.

More time passed, and I began to get nervous at the absolute stillness of Jade and Talon.

Should it take this long? I asked Dominic in our special way.

I have no idea, he answered truthfully. *I've never seen this done.*

Chewing my lip nervously, I watched as the shadowman continued to groan in pain. Minutes slipped by as he grew more agitated, raking at his scalp with his nails. Pity welled up inside me, and I could understand why Jade was set on helping these creatures. They were devastating to watch.

More time passed, and we remained unmoved. Twenty minutes, half an hour, and still, nothing but the sporadic mewling of the man on the ground.

With a gasp, Jade's eyes suddenly popped open, and she collapsed to the ground.

Talon was there, sweeping her into his arms before she had a chance to touch the floor. Before I could think, I rushed to them, reaching out for Jade.

"Is she all right?"

"No," Talon said starkly. "I'm not sure what happened, but it wasn't as before."

He turned to look down at the shadowman briefly, anger and resentment clear on his handsome features.

"He is wholly evil," his words came out barely above a whisper.

The shadowman lifted his head then, a maniacal laugh escaping that froze me to my core.

Talon gave Dominic one loaded look, and before I realized it, I was swept up and well outside the building. As he set me on my feet, I gulped in deep breaths of fresh air.

On the ground, Talon had Jade draped across his lap, one hand on her cheek. "Wake, love, wake for me," he beseeched her.

Her eyes fluttered open, much to all of our relief, and she gazed lovingly into Talon's eyes.

"Campfires and evergreens," she whispered, and it brought out a smile on Talon's face.

Dominic and I exchanged a look, and I shrugged.

"I'm okay, I promise," Jade spoke louder now, struggling to stand when her fiancé held her down. She gave him a piercing look from under her lashes, and I had a feeling words were being exchanged where we couldn't hear.

Carefully, Talon stood with Jade still in his arms, before setting her gently on her feet. She swayed just slightly, and Talon refused to relinquish the grip around her waist.

"Well, that was new," Jade attempted to make light of the situation.

"What, exactly, happened?" Dominic finally asked.

"There was no goodness in him," Jade squeezed her eyes shut, fighting back the demons she so clearly saw. "Not one speck for me to find. It was horrible."

The affect this had on her was profound. I could only imagine, as an empath, how touching pure evil must have taken its toll.

"Jade needs to rest, and recover." Talon looked to Dominic now. "He will need to be taken care of."

With a nod, Dominic took my hand again, leading me back to the car.

"We'll see you soon," Jade assured me with a smile when I hesitated.

"Take care of yourself," I told her sternly before allowing Dominic to drag me away.

When we were back in the car, heading in the direction of my house, I remained silent for a long while. There was a lot to sift through, and I took my time.

Finally, quietly, I asked the question I already knew the answer to.

"You'll kill him, won't you?"

Dominic looked over to me, but I was staring out the window, refusing to meet his gaze.

"Yes," he eventually answered, just as quietly.

I nodded, and went back to staring silently. The roads were deserted this time of night, and I dully wondered what time it actually was. When I finally turned my head towards the clock, I realized it was 3:00 in the morning. Time for lunch.

Dominic turned into my driveway, using his speed to open my door for me. He offered me his hand, which I accepted gratefully. Pulling me out of the car, he walked with me to the door, pausing on the steps.

Turning, I met his eyes for the first time since we'd left the shadowman. He was one step below me, so we were even in height and I could look directly into the glittering depths of his emerald eyes. As always, I found myself being sucked into his gaze, my body slowly shifting forward. This time, I didn't resist. There was no one to interrupt as our lips grew inexorably closer.

When they met, I let loose all the emotion I felt piling up inside me, wrapping my arms around his neck, digging my hands into his hair. Gripping chunks of his hair in my fists, I leaned into him, pouring everything I felt, everything I was, into the kiss. His arms wrapped around my waist, encouraging the closeness. Our tongues danced and the only air I breathed was that which he supplied.

With a gasp we broke apart, sucking in breaths as I attempted to slow my racing heart. We stared into each other's eyes for a long moment, saying without words what was in our hearts.

"Come back to me," I whispered on a breath.

"Always," he replied.

Releasing his hold on me, he took a step down, and then another. In a blink, he was gone.

Searching the darkness for a little while longer, knowing I'd never see him in his lightning speed, I finally turned and walked inside. The whole night felt like a dream, equal parts fantasy and nightmare. For a moment, I thought back to the first days I'd met Dominic, and my outrageous reactions to him. In particular, the moment I'd run into the forest, fool-heartedly believing I could escape my own feelings.

They were back, and stronger than ever. Only now, it wasn't a question.

I was completely, helplessly, head over heels in love with Dominic Drake.

I lay restlessly in bed, dawn just beginning to break, when I felt more than heard the intruder.

A rough hand brushed against my cheek, and a long, hard body slid into bed beside me. Sighing into the embrace, I lay my head against his chest, feeling at peace for the first time since he'd left.

"Are you all right?" He asked softly, brushing my hair away from my face.

"Now I am," I answered dreamily. "Are you all right?"

"Now I am," he replied, and I could feel his lips curl against my forehead.

His hand trailed down my side, finding the hem of the long t-shirt I'd thrown on to sleep. Once he reached my thigh, the hand began moving back up again, under the fabric.

"You're not wearing anything under this shirt," his voice whispered across my skin.

"No, I'm not," I answered.

"Naughty girl," he feathered kisses across my face, dipping to continue the assault on my neck, nuzzling the shirt aside to nip along my shoulder.

My body was alive with need, and I arched into him and his wandering hands.

"Will it ever be enough?" I wondered aloud, beginning my own exploration.

"I hope not," he answered with a growl, pulling the shirt over my head.

We came together to push the darkness away, to sate a need, to feel alive. No longer afraid of my feelings for him, I poured everything I had into every kiss, every touch. He responded to everything I gave two-fold, pushing me to a level I hadn't known existed. As my body ripped apart, lights flickered then shattered, raining glass down upon our connected forms.

CHAPTER 19

Going back to work felt odd after a day of bliss. Dominic and I had spent the majority of it in bed, sometimes eating take-out Dominic happily ordered, sometimes not. That is, after we cleaned up the mess of exploded lightbulbs.

After that event, I couldn't really deny that I might have some kind of power. For now, though, those thoughts were pushed to the back of my mind. I wanted to enjoy Dominic, without all the supernatural nonsense creeping in. We'd have to deal with that soon enough.

I'd checked on Jade sometime in the early evening, wanting to make sure she'd recovered. She assured me she had, and invited Dominic and me to join them for dinner the next night. Dominic didn't seem excited about it, but I knew he would acquiesce.

Dominic had left for Wilson's about half an hour before me, reminding me I could contact him instantly if something happened. I'd rolled my eyes at his worry, even if it was warranted.

Gabi spotted me immediately upon entering the store, greeting me in her usual bubbly way. It took me a moment to rewind the events of the last 24 hours and ask her a question that made sense.

"Did you have fun with Pearl?" I asked her.

"So much fun! I'm sorry you had to leave early," she frowned at me. "Are you feeling better?"

Hesitating for a moment, wondering what Jade had told her, I nodded. "Yup, all better."

Pausing before we split off to our different sections of the store, Gabi studied me intently. "You look different."

Before I could stop them, my eyes widened. "What do you mean?"

"I don't know," Gabi put a finger to her lips. "You just look... happy."

Shrugging this off, I answered, "I am happy."

As I walked away, Gabi watched me with narrowed eyes. For all her ditzy nature, she could be very observant. I'd have to watch myself, at least for the time being.

Heading to the prep room, I spotted Kade and Ricky, giving them a little wave as I approached.

"I'll take the freezer," Ricky said, pulling on his layers in silence.

"Great, thanks, Ricky," I answered him. He still wasn't very talkative, though we'd worked together several times. Once he plodded off down the hall, I turned to Kade. "What's your poison?"

"I'll handle dairy if you've got these two," he gestured towards the doors in front of us. "Anything new I should know about?"

For a moment I stuttered, before realizing he was asking about Gabi, or other gossip. He didn't know about Dominic.

"Not really," I told him, shrugging into my jacket. "Gabi's still seeing Ian, surprisingly."

"That's not much fun," he grumbled on his way out the door.

Laughing to myself, I pulled open the produce door and stepped inside. Though the work was monotonous, I couldn't help the small smile that continuously hovered on my lips.

As I was finishing my batch, the door pulled open. Glancing up, expecting Kade, I was pleasantly surprised by my visitor.

A wide smile on my lips, I stood in the middle of the cooler, drinking in the sight of him. "Hi."

He grinned back. "Hi."

Then, he closed the distance, pushing my back against the racks of fruit, and kissed me. My mind immediately blanked, my hands pulling him closer against me.

He broke the kiss first, leaning back to take a good look at me. "It had been too long," he said by way of explanation.

With a laugh, I slapped at his arm. "It's been less than two hours."

"Exactly," he answered gravely.

Reaching up to him on my toes, I placed a lingering kiss on his lips. "There," I told him, sinking back to the floor. "That should hold you."

"Doubt it," he growled, and I shivered in delight. Leaning close, he whispered in my ear. "Meet me in the pillow aisle at lunch."

With every inch of my body reacting to his words, I simply nodded. He placed his lips against my neck, and I moaned.

Until lunch.

He left, his words lingering on my mind, his touch on my skin. Finishing my batches in a daze, I walked to the floor, completely unaware of anyone around me. It continued on like that until break time, where I sat with Gabi, along with Noah and Becca. They were talking, but I couldn't concentrate on the flow of conversation. Not when every fiber of my being alerted me to the fact that Dominic was in the same room.

Sandra, Jacob and Dominic stood for our nightly meeting, and I used the excuse to drink him in. His eyes only flicked to me once, but a wealth of emotion poured over me.

Stop looking at me like that.

Doing my best not to give a reaction, I responded to him. *Like what?*

Like you're picturing me without my clothes on.

But I am.

A groan was my only answer. I smirked.

As lunch inched closer, I became more jumpy, barely able to contain myself. When 3:00 finally hit, I snuck off down the backroom, to the aisle Dominic had indicated. It wasn't far from the cooler, and just before the unloading area for the truck. Peeking around to make sure I was alone, I headed down the aisle. When I reached the end, an arm snaked out and yanked me around a short corner, effectively hiding us from sight of any passerby's.

"I didn't know this was here," I whispered.

"The cameras don't reach back here," Dominic rose a brow, and it was all I needed.

Yanking him against me, our mouths fused together. He lifted me from my waist, and I wrapped my legs around his. Perching me against the edge of a shelf, Dominic's hands were quickly under my shirt.

"Ugh, I forgot about this confounded suit," he complained. It made me laugh, but then his hands continued to travel up and I was distracted once again.

Wait, his voice was urgent in my mind. All activity stilled. He pushed up against me, holding us both steady.

Listening for whatever it was that had alerted Dominic, I heard heels against the floor, leading towards the large truck doors. A door opened, and we looked at each other in confusion.

The doors are supposed to be locked all night.

Do you think this has to do with the shadowman you've been chasing?

His head shook, his eyes boring into mine. *I'm not sure. Stay here.*

Before I cold protest, he was gone. As I adjusted my clothing back to respectable, he was back. "Whoever it was is gone."

Sighing, I knew our moment had passed. "I better get to the breakroom, or Gabi might just call the police."

He traced a lazy line from my neck to the top of my shirt, dipping down into my cleavage. "Mind if I come over after work?"

"You better," I blew out a breath. Giving him one more chaste kiss, I walked away.

When I got to the breakroom, Gabi waved me down.

"Sorry," I told her, sinking into the chair beside her. "Had to get some food back before it went bad."

"It's all good," she told me, then dived into a story about Ian.

Dominic never came to the breakroom, and I began to wonder what he was doing.

Who wears heels while working overnights? His voice was suddenly in my mind.

Taking a look around, I realized Sandra wasn't in the breakroom, and neither was Jake. *Only one person I can think of.*

Sandra, we thought at the same time.

What exactly do you think is going on?

There was a long pause while I waited for his answer.

A shadowman is running a drug operation out of this store, but in the two months I've been investigating, I haven't found who he has working as his puppet. This may be the closest I've come.

Pondering that, I took another good look around the room, using my observation skills to put together a list of people who seemed shady to me.

From that point on, I knew I'd have to keep my eyes open, my senses on alert. Daydreaming about Dominic could wait until after we caught the shadowman he was after.

When I left lunch, I walked the long way around to stop in the clothing department. Passing by the front where I would sit with Jordan, I said hello to Rosa, who was just cleaning up from her own meal.

She stared at me a long time, then walked closer, holding my hand as she had done before, covering it with both of hers. Her eyes gazed into mine until it became awkward.

"What is it?" I asked her in Spanish.

"The man you are with. He is not like us."

Startled, I tried to pull my hand back, but her grip only tightened.

"He is a good man, but he chases demons. The demons chase you, too."

"What do you mean?"

"Be careful," she warned, then turned abruptly, releasing my hand and walking away.

Watching her walk away, I quickly snapped myself out of my daze and made my way to softlines. Jordan and Anita were both there, and they greeted me happily.

"How's everything going?" I asked them both.

"Did you hear?" Anita stepped closer, dropping her voice.

My heart sped. Did she have something useful?

"No, what?"

"I heard Jake was dating someone that works here," she dropped the hot gossip like it was a baked potato.

Biting my lip to avoid saying anything incriminating, I responded, "Really? Wonder who."

"I've got an idea," Anita paused dramatically. "It's gotta be Kris."

Seeing Jordan roll her eyes behind Anita's back, I struggled to keep my face straight. "Yeah, maybe. I'll let you know if I hear anything."

Anita grinned at this and bounced away.

Jordan was watching me, and I turned my attention towards her. "What is it?"

"Nothing," she shrugged. "You just look different."

That was twice tonight. "I'm running on a couple of hours of sleep, so it's probably just loopy-ness you're seeing," I averted her question, then asked one of my own as a distraction. "Hey, I know you're pretty observant. Does anyone here rub you the wrong way?"

She tipped her mouth into a sardonic smile. "Plenty of people."

Though I smiled back, I waited for her to answer the question.

She sighed. "I've noticed some people sneaking off to the backroom during lunch break. They come out the main door, pass right by me like they're going to use the bathroom, but go to the back instead."

"Can you tell me who?"

"If you tell me why," she countered.

Chewing my lip, I considered. "If you promise not to say anything," I told her, knowing I could trust her not to. "Some things have gone missing from the electronics department in the back. Jake asked me if I'd seen anything, since I'm back there all the time now for PMDF. And now, I'm way too curious to let it go."

Jordan considered this, and I hoped I'd lied convincingly enough. It seemed to have worked, so she leaned even closer.

"Becca, James, Jesse, Ricky, Sandra, and..." her eyes cut to the side, judging if we were alone. She dropped her voice again. 'Anita."

Sandra was on the list. I gulped, thanked Jordan and promised to let her know if I found anything out. Of course, a couple of the names on that list bothered me. Becca, for one. We'd come to a friendship of sorts after a rocky beginning. Jesse, for another. He was one of my favorite people here.

When I got back to the coolers, I reached out to Dominic, telling him about my conversation with Jordan.

I'll look into it, he promised. *Be careful who else you talk to.*

I know who to trust, I shot back. I got the sense that he was smirking at me, but it could have also just been my imagination.

When I finally got home that morning, I took a shower to wash off the grime of the night. I wasn't sure what time Dominic would be coming over, so I threw a frozen lasagna in the oven and sat down at my computer while it warmed. There was a lot I had to rethink now for the novel, and I began the arduous task of editing, making sure I kept my vampire as far from the truth as I could. Just when I had started writing new material, there was a polite knock on the door.

Smiling, I opened it to find Dominic waiting on the steps, one hand behind his back. He brought it around to the front, presenting a fresh bouquet of flowers.

My heart fluttered in my chest at his thoughtfulness. "Oh, Dominic, thank you," I gushed, accepting the flowers and pulling him inside to give him a proper greeting.

As his hands began to wander, I quickly remembered I was wearing a robe, and only a robe. I pulled away, wanting to put the flowers in water.

"What smells so good?" He asked, following me into the tiny kitchen.

"Lasagna," I told him, pulling a vase down from a top shelf. Filling it with water from the tap, I turned to study him. "What have you found out?"

"I'll fill you in while we eat. There's something else I'd like to do first."

Before I could react, his arms were wrapped around my waist, my feet raised off the floor. The bedroom was too far, so he lifted me onto the counter, the robe's tie falling open in the process. It didn't bother me at all.

CHAPTER 20

"Do we have to go?"

Dominic was standing in my bathroom doorway, watching as I applied mascara to my lashes. Though he was still wearing jeans, I'd talked him into a dressy black button-down shirt. I was wearing a black dress with splashes of giant red flowers strewn across it.

"Yes," I told him, switching to my hair. Attempting to swirl it into a French knot, I settled for a low bun. "It'll be good for you to socialize."

"I talked to you all day," he reminded me.

"You used your mouth, but you definitely weren't always talking," I corrected him.

He moved silently to stand behind me, his hands resting lightly against my stomach. Our eyes met in the mirror, and for no reason, I found myself flushing.

"I could distract you into forgetting this dinner," he suggested.

"No," I was firm. Turning, I linked my hands behind his neck. "It will be fun, I promise."

Meeting his lips with mine, I broke it off before we could get carried away.

"Let's go, I'm driving."

"I think not," he grabbed the keys from my hand. "If you're forcing me to go, I get to drive."

Jumping for the keys, I gave up and crossed my arms. "Fine, you can drive."

He smiled triumphantly. We walked to the car, hand in hand, and I waited while he politely opened my door.

"Thank you," I said primly, slipping into the seat.

After shutting the door, he was sliding into the driver's side practically instantaneously.

Shaking my head, I scolded him. "Someone could see you."

"No one's around. I checked."

Shaking my head, I decided not to argue.

We were headed to a restaurant in the heart of downtown, and as we drove down the large hill, I sat back and enjoyed the breathtaking view of the lake as it finally came into view. The sun was low on the horizon, though we still had some time before it fully set. During this time of year, the sun graced us with its presence before 5:00 in the morning, and shone long past 9:00 at night. It was a nice trade off to the winter, when it was daylight for less than eight hours, if it shone at all.

Though I was still technically an employee at Wilson's until August, I now had no idea what else my future had in store. Would I stay here, near Dominic? Would he come with me, to my next venture? Or, would we end up somewhere completely new?

He was close to catching the shadowman, I could feel it. Earlier today, he'd told me what he'd found out, which was virtually nothing. He's used his 'tricks,' as he called it, talking to Sandra, but she seemed clueless.

Once he had done what he had come here to do, Dominic would be moving on.

Then, a more terrifying thought nudged the back of my mind- was I in his future at all?

"What are you thinking about?" Dominic asked, reaching over to clasp my hand.

"The future," I replied without thinking. Glancing up at him, I looked quickly away again.

"What about it?" He asked, his brow knitting.

"We can talk about it later," I hedged, suddenly unsure about a myriad of things. Though he looked like he wanted to push the issue, we were close to our destination and he backed off.

The restaurant was set on the water and boasted Italian fare. Remembering one of my first assessments of Duluth, I realized I had been wrong- there were Italian restaurants. Even if the food was subpar, I would take it for the view our table offered.

Jade and Talon, along with Pearl, were already sitting at one of the tables along the windows. Jade jumped up to hug me, and to my relief, Dominic shook Talon's hand. When I introduced him to Pearl, she shook his hand politely then turned to me.

"Nice work," she stage whispered.

"He can hear you," I spoke quietly back.

"Oh, I know," she craned her head around and winked at Dominic.

He seemed overly pleased by her assessment.

"Jade told me you have something like seven kids," I casually changed the subject. "How are you handling being away from them?"

"Oh, it's great," she grinned. "But I miss them like crazy."

She pulled out her phone, flipping to a picture of two babies that looked no more than six months old. "Especially these two," Pearl sighed. "But, I'm headed home in the morning."

"Wow, twins?" I asked. Pearl nodded, then showed me a picture with all seven beautiful children. "This is Ashton, Aspen, Ewan, Ella, Kalia, and the twins, Hazel and Perrin."

"Those are unusual names," Dominic piped up.

"They're all named for trees," Pearl explained. "We have a thing for themes in our family. Our older sister's names are Amber and Emerald."

"That's really neat," I told her. "My family didn't have any traditions." Unless you counted not being around.

"I'm really going to miss all the kids," Jade spoke up.

"We'll be back soon," Talon reassured her. His arm was around her back, seeming to always need the contact to his fiancé.

"Your girlfriend has been inconsolable," Pearl rolled her eyes before speaking directly to Dominic and me. "Ella, my daughter, is in love with Talon."

"Who can blame her?" Jade asked, smiling up at the object of our conversation. "He reads her princess stories."

"I'm also very cuddly," Talon pointed out.

It was Jade's turn to roll her eyes, but the love shining in them softened any ill-content.

Pearl checked the time, looking nervously at the door. "I wonder what's holding Kate up."

"Well, she is driving cross country," Jade pointed out. "We have to cut her some slack."

"You talked to her this morning, right?"

Jade nodded. "She sounded a little off, but told me she would be here. Along with someone she's driving with."

Pearl leaned forward on her elbows. "Oh, who is this mystery person? A man?"

"She didn't say," Jade grinned. "Actually, she didn't go into details at all. Okay, I'm a little worried about her, too."

You didn't say we were meeting more *people*, Dominic's voice popped into my head.

I didn't know, I told him. *You can't tell me you're not enjoying their conversation.*

A little, he finally admitted. *Pearl seems to be a bright, intuitive woman.*

It was my turn to roll my eyes. I caught Jade watching me, a small smile playing at her lips. Lifting a shoulder up and letting it drop, it was my way of saying '*men, what can you do?*'

Drinks were brought out, along with a few appetizers. I picked at a few things, and Jade dug in like she hadn't eaten for weeks. Talon and Pearl didn't seem to notice, so that must be how she normally eats.

"How long should we wait to order?" Pearl asked.

"I'll try to give Kate a call again," Jade told her, excusing herself from the table. She stepped outside the restaurant, and I could see her pacing through the front windows.

My eyes drifted back out to the lake, and the view of the lift bridge Duluth was famous for. In all the times I'd walked down here in the mornings, I still hadn't seen a ship come through.

"What are you watching?" Dominic asked me.

195

"The bridge," I motioned towards it. "I want to see one of the big ships fit through there. Seems like it would be a tight squeeze."

"Isn't this place gorgeous?" Pearl sighed. "I don't think you could ever get used to the size of that lake."

"It's like living on the ocean, except for the pesky hot weather," I commented.

Pearl grinned at me. "That's right, Gabi told me you're not from around here. How do you like it?"

"More than I ever thought I would," I answered honestly.

Outside, I spotted a woman with bright red hair approach Jade. This must be Kate. Beside her, a man joined them. He was outrageously attractive, just like Talon and Dominic, with dark, side swept hair and a stature that managed to look simultaneously menacing and helpless.

Talon's head snapped around, and after mumbling an excuse, he left the table. Dominic's body had stiffened, and I saw that he was staring outside.

What is it?

Stay here. Distract Pearl.

"Excuse me," Dominic spoke aloud. Then, he was gone.

Wide eyes turned to Pearl, and I struggled to control my racing heart. Something was going on, and it couldn't be good.

"Was it something I said?" Pearl joked.

Focusing on her, I managed to smile. "Not sure what that was about. So, tell me what Sun Valley is like. I've never lived in a town so small."

196

"You'd be surprised at how great it is! I don't think I could stand to live in a big city. Even something like Duluth, it never interested me."

"But, what is there to do? How do you go shopping?"

Pearl laughed. "Our kind of fun is different, for sure. My husband and older kids got into dirt biking last year, and started up again as soon as the snow cleared. We do a lot of family dinners, backyard barbeques and camp fires. It's the kind of place that, if you're not related to your neighbor, you at least know who they are."

I shook my head in amazement, sneaking a look outside. It looked like the five were in a heated discussion, but at least it hadn't turned violent.

"As for shopping, we just have to plan in advance and make a day trip out of going to one of the bigger towns around us. Also, the internet is amazing."

With that, I had to agree.

Our group walked in then, and Pearl jumped up to hug her cousin. She looked so similar to Jade and Pearl, they could have been sisters. They all had the same bright green eyes, easily pegging their heritage as Irish, but Kate's vibrant hair made her stand out even in this crowd.

Dominic came to my side as I stood to greet the new arrivals, wrapping an arm around my waist.

Kate turned to me, shaking my hand, then introducing her driving companion.

"This is Hugh," she told us.

When his dark gaze landed on me, I felt an instant connection to him, though I'd never met him before. Not like my connection to Dominic, more like I felt when I first saw Jade or Talon.

He's an Elemental, Dominic confirmed in my mind.

"Nice to meet you," I stuttered, grasping the proffered hand.

Hugh took a seat beside Pearl, in the corner with a view of the entire restaurant. His searching gaze never settled in one spot. Though it made him seem detached, I recognized it for what it was.

He was running from someone.

We ordered dinner, the table full of tension. Kate and Pearl chatted animatedly, but the rest of us remained shrouded in silence. Though I desperately wanted to know what was going on, Dominic wasn't forthcoming with information.

Are we in danger? I finally asked.

He hesitated. *I'm not sure.*

That was helpful.

After dinner, Jade is going to make sure Pearl gets back to their hotel safely, and then we will be having a discussion with all of them.

I glanced again at Kate, who looked stressed under her smiles, and Hugh, who was still searching the room as if he expected a raid at any moment. It was subtle, but I could tell in his body language how protective he was of Kate. From what I'd gleaned from Jade and Pearl, they'd only just met, and it made me only more curious about their story.

Our food arrived, and I picked half-heartedly at my mushroom ravioli. Jade packed away her meal, eating with as much gusto as she had the appetizers. I was in awe of her appetite.

Talon spied me watching, and grinned conspiratorially. "She's always like this."

Jade paused with the fork halfway to her mouth, still chewing her previous bite. "What?"

We all laughed. Hugh even twitched a smile, and in that aspect, he reminded me of Dominic.

Swallowing what was in her mouth, Jade spoke again. "I'm from Wisconsin. I like to eat."

"Yeah, so am I, and I've never eaten like you," Pearl joined in.

Shrugging, Jade ripped off another chunk of bread. "I've got a good metabolism."

The moment of levity helped ease some of the tension, and we finished our meal on a lighter note.

As we left the restaurant, Talon spoke briefly to Dominic before they all left, heading back to their hotel. Dominic led me away from where we'd parked, onto the lake walk. Since that was one of my favorite pastimes, I didn't complain.

We walked at a leisurely pace, winding our way closer to the lift bridge. Once we were standing right beside it, I realized there was a ship, one of the salties, not too far out and pointed this direction.

"There's a ship coming in," Dominic explained, pausing at the dock wall. "You said you'd like to see it."

Excitement coursed through me.

"Thank you," I told him, reaching up to kiss his cheek.

Forgetting the drama of Kate and Hugh for the moment, I watched with delight as the bridge sounded its warning before shutting off traffic of cars and pedestrians from crossing. As the ship neared, passing the lighthouse at the end of the pier, the bridge itself lifted to the sky. There was a small building built into the top of the bridge, which Dominic leaned close to explain a guard sat up there, ensuring people remained safe while ships passed.

As the ship inched closer, it suddenly sounded one long horn, which made me jump, followed by two short blasts. Dominic's hand was steady at my back, his amused laughter in my ear. The bridge now in top position, the ship sailed smoothly under. When I looked straight forward, I could only see a wall of solid metal. It seemed there were mere inches to each side of the canal that weren't filled.

Several minutes passed as the ship stayed steady on its course. Tiny windows above revealed smiling faces of the crew, and I waved up at them. Once the ship was well past the bridge, it began to lower again, the same bells sounding. The ship gave another salute, and the smile on my face refused to diminish.

Crowds of people that had gathered to watch began to disperse, and I turned to Dominic. "That was amazing!"

"I'm glad you liked it," he responded before steering me away from the crowd.

As we made our way back to our parked car, I finally asked the questions burning in my mind.

"Who is Hugh? Who is he running from?"

Dominic sighed, glancing down at me. "Hugh is an Elemental who has lost his memory. He believes he was drugged by a group of humans who is hunting our kind. Jade is going to attempt to help him."

CHAPTER 21

As Dominic drove me to the meeting spot, his hand wrapped around mine, I traced the symbols on his arm.

"What do your tattoos mean?" I asked.

"They are symbols from Elemental spells," he told me.

My eyes shot to his, surprised. That hadn't been what I was expecting.

"From what my parents explained, Elementals have origins in every culture. Native Americans, like Talon, or Irish, like Jade. If you look closely enough, you can find a trace of magic any place you look. We believe, at one time, all Elementals were more closely connected than we are now. Whether because we have become scarcer, or because we, like everything else on this earth, succumbs to evolution, many of the old ways have been lost."

He paused then, glancing down at me, for I was abnormally quiet.

"Go on," I encouraged, still running a finger lightly over the runes.

"Knowledge was shared, but with so many different cultures, and, therefore, languages, Elementals created their own language. This," he gestured along his arms, "is the language of my people."

"That's amazing," I breathed, studying the lines more carefully. "It's too bad so much has been lost."

Dominic shrugged. "It's the way of the world."

Though that was a bit depressing, the fact that we were meeting with a group of others like him was inspiring.

We remained silent after that, and I traded my time between studying Dominic and watching our surroundings. I didn't know where we were going, and hadn't bothered to ask. We were headed north and slightly to the east, houses quickly falling away to forest.

Dominic turned down several dirt roads, until finally we left even those to nothing more than a trail. Trees towered along either side of us, my car barely scraping past. Eventually, the space opened up to reveal a small cabin, the trees forming a protective barrier over the top.

"Where are we?" I asked, staring ahead. Next to the cabin was a single garage, but there was no sign of life.

"My home," Dominic answered me.

"It's very… secluded," I finished, not sure what else to say. When I'd imagined where Dominic spent his downtown, this hadn't been the picture I'd conjured.

"It's preferable for my way of life," he answered cryptically. "I offered my home as a protected place for Jade to assist Hugh."

"That was very nice of you," I swallowed once, then met his gaze. "You'll turn into a socialite yet."

"Don't count on it," he muttered, and I grinned at him. Stepping close, I waited for him to lean down and press his lips to mine.

We heard another vehicle approach, so we broke apart but remained linked by our hands.

Talon, Jade, Kate and Hugh all exited the SUV. Jade walked right up to us without hesitation, but I could see Hugh's caution plainly on his face. Though I didn't think she knew it, Kate was very attuned to him, and it made me wonder again what, exactly, their connection was.

"Thanks for inviting us out here," Jade smiled easily. "You have a beautiful property."

"Thank you," Dominic responded pleasantly.

He turned then, leading me and the rest of the party to the front door. When I stepped inside, the décor was more of what I had expected from a man like Dominic. The living room consisted of a black leather couch and a wide screen TV, and one bookshelf with just a few items on it. Directly behind the couch was the open kitchen, with stainless steel appliances and a small island with a couple of stools. The space beside the kitchen had a square table with four chairs. There was no clutter on any of the counter or table space, no frills of any kind.

A hallway to the left held three doors which were closed, and I assumed that would lead to his bedroom and a bathroom, and maybe an office space or storage. Perhaps, once everyone left, I would get a tour.

Jade settled on the thick carpet in front of the couch, Talon at her back. Hugh sat opposite her, and Kate sat on the couch, near enough to place an encouraging hand on Hugh's back.

"I will watch over you all," Dominic assured them.

Together, we moved towards the kitchen, wanting to give them space to do whatever it was they were doing. I perched on a stool, feeling a bit out of place.

203

"When we did this with our friend Lani, it took several hours, though it didn't seem that long to either Jade or Lani," Talon announced as a warning to all of us.

Hugh glanced to Kate, a wealth of emotion shared in a simple look. Feeling like an intruder on a private moment, I snuck my hand inside Dominic's, pulling him down beside me. The only warning we had to them beginning was Jade's eyes slipping closed, Hugh's following shortly after.

It was completely silent in the room. Talon had also closed his eyes in concentration, and Kate didn't move, not breaking her link with the mysterious man.

Dominic and I sat and watched for a long time, but they were unmoving. Even Kate remained as a statue, which was impressive. I could already feel my back beginning to ache. After an hour, I stood quietly and stretched, then remained standing to give my back a break. Dominic pulled me in front of him, and I leaned into him, enjoying the feel of his arms wrapped around me. That was a much more comfortable position than sitting had been.

Another half an hour ticked by, and without warning, Jade's eyes shot open. Talon's and Hugh's followed, and they all remained glued in place, blinking at each other. I could only imagine what they had seen, and how difficult it must be to re-orient back to reality.

"What happened?" Kate asked first, barely able to contain herself.

"We've uncovered one fact," Hugh sagged with relief at having just one piece to the puzzle slide into place. "Everything else was just... a blur."

Jade nodded her agreement. "Blurry, but not black. I think, with time, your memories will return to you. For now, at least you have the one thing to go on."

"What is it?" Kate asked again.

Hugh looked at her a long time before answering. "I know what I was doing before I was caught."

We were all silent, waiting for more. Kate was the first to speak.

"What were you doing?"

Hugh glanced to Talon, then over to Dominic. Something was shared between the men that I couldn't quite grasp.

"There is a group that is hunting our kind. They don't differentiate between the shadowmen and Elementals. They capture and torture whomever they believe to be supernatural. The majority of their captives are innocents."

One of his hands tightened into a fist, and I watched as Kate sank to the floor beside him, giving him a lifeline in the depth of the brutal images he was now seeing.

He calmed visibly, then continued. "I'm not sure how I found out about these camps, but I remember working to shut them down. They've developed a serum that can incapacitate our kind. That's what I was shot with, and what has caused me to lose my memories. I managed to escape, but with no memory, I didn't even know where to run to."

205

Jade spoke up now. "We are heading out to the southwest anyway, so we will come with you to California. It will give you extra protection, and we can work on your memories more."

"Lani is working to find others of our kind," Talon added. "Perhaps we can uncover who is behind these torture camps. It would also be nice to find a healer."

"What's a healer?" I asked.

Talon turned to me, explaining the best he could. "Many of our people have abilities that go beyond element manipulation. Healers are similar to doctors, but more. From what my mother told me, they are able to connect their spirit to the person who is ill, and heal them from the inside out."

"That sounds incredible," I breathed. The more I learned, the more questions I had.

"Unfortunately, so much of our culture has been lost. Dominic, I wanted to ask you of the symbols on your arms. These look familiar to me, I believe my mother used them."

Uncomfortable being the center of attention, Dominic briefly explained what he had told me in the car. Jade and Talon shared a look. Hugh seemed interested in the conversation, but without his memories, he had no real connection to any of it.

"We need to rebuild," Jade finally commented. "No one should spend so many years alone." Here, she squeezed Talon's hand, then continued. "It seems Elementals could be such a force for good. We need to find as many as we can, figure out a way to reconnect."

206

"It is easier said than done, but I agree wholly," Talon threw his support behind Jade.

"As do I," Dominic surprised me by speaking. "I have a twin brother, who is hunting a shadowman in Europe. Before we became hunters, we were inseparable, and happy. Our parents taught us much of the old ways, while also ignoring their own gifts. It was their downfall. We can prevent that from happening to others. Allow our children to grow in a safe, happy environment."

I was stunned. Partly by his speech, but more so the meaning behind his words. All the dreams I'd had since moving to Duluth suddenly became clear. The gray wolf was Dominic. The red-brown wolf was his brother.

Ignoring that fact for a moment, my focus went to the last of his statement. Our children. Did he mean me and him? Or children in general?

Swallowing once, I shoved those thoughts to the back. What he had said was beautiful, and for now, I would leave it at that.

"You can turn into a wolf," my voice came out barely above a whisper. "You, and your brother. Gray and red-brown wolves."

Dominic stared at me, dumbfounded. Forgetting we were not alone in the room, he took both of my hands carefully in his. "How do you know that?"

"I… I dreamt it."

After several beats of silence, Jade finally interrupted. "You connected to his memories," she said gently. "I did the same with Talon."

Staring at her for a moment, I switched my gaze back to Dominic. With so much information swirling in my brain, there was one vital piece desperately attempting to form. When I tried again to latch on to it, it managed to slip through.

Once everyone had left, I had Dominic all to myself. The group of four would be leaving in the morning, but I now had contact information for both Jade and Kate. Once things calmed down, I knew I would be peppering Jade with questions nonstop.

Wrapping my arms around Dominic's waist, I pressed my face against his chest.

"This is really nice," I commented.

"What's that?" He asked.

"Just being here, with you."

Though I couldn't see him, I felt his smile. "Would you like to see the rest of the house?"

Nodding, I leaned back to look up at him. He was staring down at me, his eyes shining with some unnamed emotion. It took my breath away.

His mouth lowered to mine in the softest, sweetest kiss. The normal urgency and full out passion that overtook us had turned into a slow burn, filling me with something I'd never felt before.

Love, you idiot, my brain whispered to me.

Whatever it was, I only wanted more. Taking what I could and giving everything back, I didn't realize we'd moved until I was lying on my back.

Dominic broke from the kiss to look down at me, his hand cupping my cheek.

"I've been fighting this since the moment I met you. At every opportunity, I pushed you away, but I couldn't stay away. Reese, you're everything to me."

A smile broke through, and I placed my hand on the side of his face. "Dominic," I cut him off. "I love you, too."

No more words were needed. As we crashed together, for the first time in my life, I felt truly complete.

The next night was back to work like normal, and it was as I was walking out the next morning that it hit me. I'd been such an idiot.

Dominic, I spoke quickly into his mind. *The freezer!*

What?

Shoes get frozen in the freezer!

There was a beat of silence. I knew I wasn't making sense, so I continued to babble.

I was wearing a pair of boots the first time I was in the freezer, and they froze. When I walked on the cement of the back room, they sounded like heels.

You don't think it was Sandra?

No, I hesitated, then added, *Ricky was in the freezer that night.*

I'm on it, Dominic assured me.

Our connection broke, and I walked to my car with a bounce in my step. As I unlocked the door, I suddenly got the feeling I wasn't alone. Spinning, I realized there was a man standing several feet away.

Giving him a polite smile, I turned my attention back to unlocking my door. The uneasy feeling remained. Glancing over my shoulder, I found the man had glided forward.

Heart in my throat, I stared at him, knowing it was rude. "Can I help you?" I managed to stammer.

"Excuse me," his gentle voice somehow grated on my nerves. His face was composed into a careful smile. "I didn't mean to startle you. Could you give me directions to the mall?"

Relieved, I nodded, gesturing behinds me. "Sure, it's just down the street…"

When I looked back at him, he was now within a step of my personal space. Alarm bells were shrieking, but his eyes had fixed me in their gaze, and I had a difficult time thinking.

"You were saying?" He asked pleasantly.

"About a half mile," I told him, my hand waving uselessly in the direction he'd asked.

He was closer yet, though I hadn't seen him move. His hand reached out to grasp my arm, and the vile touch cleared my mind instantly.

Dominic! I cried into his mind, but it was too late. Something hard made contact with the back of my skull, and blackness descended.

CHAPTER 22

When I woke, I was uncomfortable and groggy. Nothing made sense: the smell of fresh cut wood surrounding me, the rough floor beneath me. The fact that my hands were restrained, or that I'd been asleep- none of it would connect in my brain.

With a groan, I rolled from my back to my side, my bound hands clutching against my stomach.

Forcing my eyes to open, I stared uncomprehendingly at my surroundings. It was a freshly built room, the wood of the walls still leaking sap. The floor was cold cement, and I was somehow attached to it by my feet.

"Ah, you're awake," the voice which spoke made me cringe. Feet stepped into my line of sight, and I turned my head to follow up the neatly pressed pants, to the black dress shirt, into a face I could plainly see was pure evil.

"What do you want from me?" My voice came out rough and cracked, and I had to clear it noisily.

"Call out to him," the man said.

My heartbeat sped, but I maintained an outward calm. "Who?"

"The man who has interfered with my business. Call out to him, *now*."

Several pieces of information suddenly fell into place. The man in the parking lot, the man standing before me now- he was a shadowman. The shadowman Dominic had been chasing for months.

He must be afraid of Dominic, if he didn't go after him directly. That gave me an edge, if a slight one.

213

I was his bait.

"No." From my prone position, I did my best to look stern.

Rage ignited in his eyes. Before I'd realized he'd moved, the shadowman bent down to backhand me across the face. My eyes stung from the impact, and I turned my head away to allow a tear to leak out.

"Do it! Call him now!"

Unable to speak, I merely shook my head.

The shadowman let out a growl akin to an otherworldly beast. Knowing another blow was coming, I flinched away. The impact never came.

Opening one eye, I saw the shadowman straighten, a dangerous grin on his face. He was facing the wall, seeing- or hearing- something I could not. My heart dropped. Dominic must be close.

Dominic, no, I sent a weak thread to him. *It's a trap*.

I'm coming for you, Dominic's voice was strong and infused me with strength.

Glaring up at the shadowman, I blinked and he was gone.

He was going after Dominic.

He's coming, I called out to him. My voice was stronger, but I was still trapped against the floor. Struggling to sit up, I realized my hands were held together by a zip tie. Focusing on that first, I remembered once seeing a child break zip ties, knowing there was a way to do it. Bringing my hands in front of me, I turned them so my palms faced me first, then twisted and pulled simultaneously.

It hurt, and red welts were instantly marring my skin, but it worked. The tie snapped and my hands were free.

214

Taking a careful look at my legs, I became disheartened. There were metal cuffs around each ankle, attached to a chain which was secured by a metal stake set into the cement.

There was a slim chance of picking the lock, if I could find an object that would work. My hands slipped through my hair, hoping against hope that there would be a bobby pin somewhere in the tangle.

There wasn't.

Casting about the one room cell, I saw nothing of use to me. Panic set in, tenfold, as I heard a sound like thunder just outside the wall. I rolled to my knees, bringing my hands up in a pathetic attempt at a defensive stance. It wasn't perfect, but I wasn't going down with a fight.

The loud noises continued, and I realized it wasn't a storm, but the two men fighting. Imagining the worst, I was near hysteria when, without warning, there was silence.

My eyes were on the door, anxiety nearly crippling. After several minutes, it banged open. The shadowman stood in the frame, bleeding from wounds inflicted in battle. He stared down at me like an avenging angel. Or, more accurately, a demon.

With one hand, he dragged Dominic forward and tossed him into the room like a ragdoll. He was unconscious, and from the distance we were, I couldn't be sure that he was alive.

"No!" The word torn from my very soul echoed out into the room.

The shadowman smiled, and in that moment, I wanted to rip him apart with my bare hands.

"I've brought him to you so you may die together," the shadowman said.

He lit a ball of fire in his palm with a thought, pressing it to the wall nearest him. The flames rapidly caught and spread. Somewhere in my jumble of thoughts, I had a dim awareness that fire shouldn't spread so quickly on fresh wood.

Must be magic.

With a wicked laugh, the shadowman turned to leave.

Rage filled me, starting at my core and building until my hair crackled with it. Letting loose an otherworldly scream, I directed all my thoughts to the shadowman trying to escape.

It was too late for him. The knowledge came from deep inside me, some untapped part of my soul. It didn't matter how fast he was, how powerful. He was mine.

The air itself compressed, dragging energy from the earth, the flames of the fire and the air until it swirled in a frightening eddy of power. Lightning exploded out of the vortex, straight through the shadowman's heart.

He collapsed to the ground, his lifeless eyes staring into the night.

I followed suit, the rage fueling me abruptly gone. My gaze fixed on Dominic, still lying prone on the floor.

Dragging myself to the unconscious man, I cupped his face in my hands, barely able to see through the torrent of tears.

"No," I moaned. "Please, Dominic, you need to wake up. You need to live."

Placing my forehead against his, a memory pushed itself to the forefront of my thoughts. Sleep, and blood…

Something Dominic had told me lit my world with hope.

"Our bodies can withstand more than the average human. Physical injuries which should take days to heal, will only take hours. Sleep, and an influx of blood, both speed up the process further."

This would work. It *had* to work.

If it did work, there would be only one solution left to him. In this moment, I was absolutely sure of my decision. There really was no other choice. He had to live. The world couldn't exist without him in it.

Sudden clarity left me calm. Not only was I in love with this man, he was my mate, and I would do anything to save him.

That was what he'd wanted me to discover on my own. That was the secret he'd been hiding from me. The truth that had been so obvious to Jade and Talon.

Using the dull edge of my cuff, I ripped open my own wrist. Lying beside him, I placed the jagged cut, dripping with blood, over his mouth.

"I choose you," I told him severely.

The rush of blood flowed freely into his mouth, down his throat. I must have hit an artery, I thought dully as the edges of my vision faded to black. *It has to work*, I reminded myself.

"Live," I whispered to Dominic. "Live, and then save me."

CHAPTER 23

There was pain. So much pain.

Fire ripped through me, from the tips of my fingers down to my core. I was screaming, in agony, in terror, in frustration.

I'd lost.

The fire had won. I'd been too slow, too weak to save Dominic. And now, we both burned.

It lasted longer than I thought possible. How could a body withstand such heat, such intensity without simply exploding?

Time meant nothing. It ebbed and flowed as indistinctly as a dream. But this wasn't a dream. It was a nightmare.

Once, I thought I heard a voice. An angel's voice, apologizing to me. Something cool touched my skin, but the fire quickly sucked out the cold.

Then, finally, something changed.

It got worse.

What I thought had been heat was merely a warm summer's eve. This new wave was unending and all consuming. Who I was, what I was fighting for, none of it mattered anymore. My past, present and future only consisted of one thing; burning alive.

More time went by in the endless torture. The first thought that came back to me was this: I have fingertips.

Not only that I had fingertips, but that I could *feel* them. There, at the end of my hands. Yes, I could feel those too. As each body part came into focus, relief flooded through me, cool as an autumn morning.

Something squeezed my hand again, but it wasn't cool as I remembered it being. It wasn't hot, either. It was the same as me.

The fire was slowly receding, allowing me to think for the first time since it had begun. It continued to dwindle, my chest its last holdout. My heart struggled to beat through the burning. One sludgy beat, then another. And then... silence.

No fire, and no heartbeat.

I really was dead then.

With a gasp, my eyes shot open as my heart restarted, stronger than it ever had been. Several things clicked into place simultaneously.

I was alive, and my skin was not a melted mass. Beneath me was a soft bed, and it had not been charred in the fire that had consumed me. Above me was the most beautiful view I could imagine.

"Dominic," my voice came out dry, raspy. It was the only part of me that didn't feel rejuvenated.

"Reese," he breathed out on a sigh. There was a well of emotion on his face, causing his eyes to glitter at me. They were breathtaking.

"You saved me." There was awe in my tone.

"You saved me, first," was his reply.

I cracked a smile, lifting one hand to sneak around his neck, pulling his face down to mine. It had been too long since I'd felt the softness of his lips.

Though I could have continued, there was something important I needed to say. Pulling back, I gazed at him in wonder.

"You're my mate," I stated.

"As you are mine," he responded.

Smiling contentedly, I brushed my thumb gently beneath his eye, catching a tear as it fell. To see this man cry was nearly my undoing.

"What's wrong?"

He shook his head, unable to speak for a moment. "I thought I'd lost you."

Thinking for a moment, I answered, "There were a few moments that gave me pause, as well."

That earned me a smile, and on seeing it, my heart nearly exploded with love.

Struggling to sit up, I glanced around myself. I was in Dominic's bed, and a look at the window told me it was dark outside. Dominic handed me a glass of water, which I swallowed in three large gulps.

Finished, I asked, "How long have I been..."

Making a vague gesture with my hand, I waited for him to fill in some gaps.

"Six days," he told me with a tortured look in his eye.

His fist tightened, and I placed a hand over it to remind him that I was fine now.

Shaking his head to clear it, he continued. " When I woke, you were nearly lifeless beside me."

He choked back the emotion that was so plain on his face.

"I knew you'd save me," I told him gently, forcing his gaze back to me.

"I still can't believe what you did."

Shrugging as if it had been no big deal, I replied, "It was our only chance to escape."

He didn't have an answer for that. "I will never let you come to harm again."

I smiled wryly. "Fine by me." After a moment's thought, I groaned. Dominic immediately began checking me for injuries. "I'm so fired."

Startled, he stared at me. "I called in for you. Well, for both of us."

"Guess we're out in the open now," I joked. "It's fine, though. I'm going to quit."

This time, he laughed. "Me, too."

"What happened with Ricky?"

Dominic sobered immediately. "He has been released from control now that the shadowman is gone," he paused here, raising a brow at me. "Which reminds me, how exactly did that happen?"

Looking down, I felt a blush begin to creep up. "Oh, that. Well, I, uh… I created lightning."

There was silence. Finally, I snuck a peak up at him, judging his reaction.

"You… created lightning."

"Yes." This time I grinned, unable to prevent the gloat.

He shook his head. "I didn't see that coming."

"Just don't tick me off in the future," I joked.

Speaking of the future… watching him carefully, I brought up the topic I'd been avoiding well before the incident with the shadowman happened.

222

"What happens now? With us?"

"Well," Dominic began, picking at an invisible thread in the comforter. "Now that you know we're mates, I was hoping... I mean, I would like..."

I'd never seen him so flustered before. Letting him off the hook, I took his hand in both of mine. "We stay together," I decided for us. "No matter where we go."

Relieved, Dominic nodded his agreement.

"Though, I had an idea about where that would be."

He cocked his head, interested in my thought.

Clearing my throat, I spoke again. "Let's go to Europe, to find your brother. You two shouldn't be apart. We can find the shadowman that killed your parents, together."

Dominic's face split into a large grin, and when his lips met mine again, I never wanted him to stop.

I'd talked Dominic into letting me go to Wilson's the next morning to quit. Though I had much to learn when it came to my powers, I felt strong enough to walk into the store and give my notice.

Besides, Dominic wouldn't be far.

The thought of beginning to learn everything about my new life was intoxicating. Especially having Dominic as my instructor; though, now that my thoughts drifted towards him, they went directly to even more pleasant things.

Perhaps learning from him wouldn't be very productive, but I would enjoy it immensely just the same.

I went to the store early enough that it was still the night managers on duty, but near the end of shifts. When I was walking in, Jordan was walking out.

"Hey!" I greeted her. "I'm glad I ran into you."

"Me, too!" She replied. "How are you feeling? We heard you came down with some weird bug."

"Much better," I told her. "But, I'm actually going in right now to give my notice."

"I figured," Jordan leaned closer to me. "So, you and Dominic, huh?"

I felt myself blush, though I wasn't sure why. "Yes," I grinned.

Leaning away again, Jordan crossed her arms and rose a brow. "I like to think I had something to do with that."

Laughing, I agreed. "You sure did."

"We'll have to keep in contact," Jordan told me.

"I would love that," I told her. "But, there's actually something I need to tell you."

Her interest piqued, Jordan remained silent, waiting for me to spill.

"I'm the writer, Valerie Reed."

There was a beat of silence, then she did something less like Jordan and more like Gabi. She squealed.

"What! That is so amazing! Wait, before you head off into the sunset with Dominic, you have to come meet my mom! Would you do that? Oh, and you have to sign our books, and…"

I cut her off, laughing at her unusual outburst. "I'd love to meet your mom. Let's plan a dinner or something, okay?"

Jordan launched forward, hugging me quickly. "You got it!"

Bidding her goodbye, I walked into the employee entrance for the last time.

By the time I was done saying my goodbyes, the store was open for business. The longest goodbye was with Gabi, who hugged me so tightly I was sure I'd cracked a rib. After assuring her we'd stay in touch, I managed to escape.

As I was walking out of the main doors, a group was coming in. Though I didn't mean to eavesdrop, with my new and improved hearing, staying out of other people's business was increasingly difficult.

"I just need diapers," a woman was saying. "You didn't both need to come with me."

"Of course we did," said a man's voice.

"Are you sure Aden can handle the babies?" Another man seemed worried.

"Yes," answered the woman, "don't you trust him?"

"Well, of course, with my life. But with babysitting…"

As was considered polite in the Midwest, I glanced over to nod my hello at the group. My eyes shifted over the two having the conversation and caught on the third.

"Hugh?" I spoke aloud before I could sensor myself. Three faces turned towards me, and I instantly felt the strange buzzing in my veins that meant only one thing: the three standing before me were Elementals.

"What did you say?" The man I'd mistaken for Hugh stepped forward aggressively. In that instant I could see my mistake; though this man was nearly identical to Hugh, they were clearly not the same person.

Taking a step back, I called out automatically for Dominic using our special connection.

The woman, a gentle smile on her face, placed a restraining hand on the man's arm and stepped forward.

"My name is Reya," she said, then gestured behind her. "This is Tristan and Jared."

"Reese," I told them.

"Nice to meet you, Reese. This is very important. Do you know Hugh?"

As always, the hair on my arms rose, announcing Dominic's arrival. He moved antagonistically ahead of me, shoving me behind him in the process. The man Reya had introduced as Tristan let out a growl, copying the movement.

Way to make friends, I spoke to Dominic privately before poking my head around him.

"This is Dominic," I introduced him, much to his annoyance.

"I'd very much like to know what you're doing here," Dominic spoke with quiet authority.

"Tristan, please, let's hear them out," the man who looked like Hugh came up to stand beside Tristan.

Dominic's eyes flicked over him, but remained silent.

The three were intimidating, much as all Elementals I'd met so far had been.

Reya took charge, stepping forward, ignoring the hard gaze of the man who was obviously her mate.

"We don't mean you any harm," she assured Dominic. "We've come here searching for Jared's brother. His name is Hugh. I think Reese may know him."

Bolstered by Reya's boldness, I stepped next to Dominic, waiting for him to meet my eyes. *I believe them. Please, stop acting like a macho man.*

Your safety is my upmost concern.

I love you, too, I smiled at him.

Turning back to Reya, I spoke aloud. "Please excuse my mate. He's overprotective, as I'm sure you understand."

She gave me a wry smile. "I know a thing or two about that." Leaning closer, she put a hand to her mouth as if she were letting me in on a secret. "There's a third one around here I have to put up with."

"That is enough joking at my expense," Tristan admonished us with a light smile, linking his hand with Reya's.

"Please," Jared spoke again, and I felt bad that we were making light of a situation that was clearly difficult for him. "My brother. You know him?"

Stealing a look up at Dominic, I answered. "Yes, we met him a little over a week ago."

"He's alive," relief flooded Jared's features, relaxing his muscles and making him look ten years younger. "Do you know where he is?"

"No," I answered him, "but we have a way to find out."

227

Dear Reader,

Thank you for reading *Night Shift: Book 3 of The Gifted Series*. I hope you enjoyed this second installment in The Gifted Series and join us in meeting the next mated pair, Kate and Hugh, in their book, *Stow Away*.

If you enjoyed this book, please visit Amazon to leave a review. It would only take a few moments and would help spread the word. A review would be greatly appreciated!

As always, you can keep up-to-date by "liking" me on Facebook, @anabannovels

Always, Ana

Other books by Ana Ban:

The Parker Grey Series

Abstraction; A Parker Grey Novel (Book 1)

Backfire; A Parker Grey Novel (Book 2)

Coercion; A Parker Grey Novel (Book 3)

Deception; A Parker Grey Novel (Book 4) (available December, 2017)

The Gifted Series

Allure of Home: Book 1 of The Gifted Series

Immaculate: Book 2 of The Gifted Series

Night Shift: Book 3 of The Gifted Series

Stow Away: Book 4 of The Gifted Series

The Mirror Trilogy

Infiltration: Book 1 of The Mirror Trilogy

Split: Book 2 of The Mirror Trilogy (available October, 2017)

Wakening: Book 3 of The Mirror Trilogy (available soon)

18938271R00143

18938271R00143

18938271R00143

18938271R00143

18938271R00143

18938271R00143

18938271R00143

18938271R00143

18938271R00143

18938271R00143

18938271R00143

18938271R00143

18938271R00143

18938271R00143

18938271R00143

18938271R00143

18938271R00143

18938271R00143

18938271R00143

18938271R00143

18938271R00143